BUTTERFLIES
AT THE WINDOW

A Story of Butterfly People
and Miracles in the Storm

A NOVEL

by SANDI MCREYNOLDS

Butterflies at the Window
By Sandi McReynolds

ISBN-13:
978-0692704295 (VineTree Press)

ISBN-10:
0692704299

VineTree Press

Author Sandi McReynolds and her family survived the F5 tornado in Joplin, MO in May 2011, and she has used her first-hand experience to write a fascinating "up close and been there" novel. Although *Butterflies at the Windows* is fiction, Sandi hasn't altered the facts. People who know Joplin can say, "Yes, that's right," as they read about the places and events in her story. She has done a remarkable job of taking a true experience and showing it through a novel.

LeAnn Campbell
Author of *Century Farm* mystery series for kids

Anyone who wants to be inspired should read *Butterflies at the Window*. Author Sandi McReynolds has taken an actual tragedy, the incredibly destructive tornado that ripped through Joplin, MO, leaving a wide swath of rubble for many miles, added the stories of butterfly people that flooded the area, and turned it into a healing fantasy. Congratulations!

Richard L. Jackson, B.A, M.A.
Assistant Vice President, Duke University
Senior Vice President, St. John's Regional Medical Center

FOR:

The Joplin Tornado survivors, whose courage and faith offer hope and triumph in the midst of tragedy;

Our favorite survivors, Carissa, Lilly, Gabriel and Kayleah, whose stories helped inspire this book;

The volunteers who came by the thousands, and still come, with help and renewal for a shattered community;

And last but certainly not least; Mac, my best friend and husband, without whose patience and encouragement this book would not have happened.

CONTENTS

ACKNOWLEDGMENTS

This story began gnawing at my heart the first time we drove through the horrifying mountains of rubble that had, only a few days before, been the core of Joplin. Then, as amazing accounts of courage and heroism emerged and sightings of "butterfly people" began to proliferate, it had to be told!

My plan was that it would be a fantasy about those intriguing butterfly people, with God's presence in the storm only metaphorical; but <u>His</u> plan is always best, and the Joplin Tornado story cannot be told—even as a fantasy—if He is not the center of it. There really is something different about Joplin because at heart her people understand that.

We are all tornado survivors. Whether our address is Joplin, MO, or one of the dozens of other communities surrounding this city where so many of us work and play and shop and doctor and worship, as our friend Denise so eloquently expressed from halfway around the world, "[We are] Joplin." Our friends are here. Our livelihoods are here. Our entertainment is here. Our churches are here. But most of all, our God is here.

Thank You, God, for writing us into Your story!

BUTTERFLIES at the WINDOW
SUNDAY MORNING, MAY 22, 2011

7:00
Southwest Joplin, MO
McConnell Home

It was going to be a good day!

Elly stretched luxuriously and lay with her eyes closed; savoring the moment. It was almost too perfect. She slowly opened one eye and smiled. Yep. Perfect sky, fresh and bright and blue with just a few fluffy white clouds. Perfect sun, warm and soft across her bed. Perfect leaves on the tree just outside her window. *Her* tree... planted by her parents the day she was born and adorned by the prayers they etched there each year on her birthday. She watched lavish green leaves sway gently in the breeze and thought about the day to come.

It was going to be a very good day!

In just a few hours she would be Erin Elizabeth McConnell, High School Graduate! Before long she would stand before the Class of 2011 in that big college auditorium and deliver her last high school speech. She'd practiced it one final time before she went to sleep last night and knew every line on every page, neatly highlighted and underlined and collated in its leather folder on her favorite chair.

Murmurs from the kitchen below brought another smile. Gran and Pops would be here for breakfast soon. She was so glad they were able to make the trip. Mom tried to hide it, but Elly knew she was concerned about Pops' heart problems. Anyway, they would be here, and the whole family would be together to celebrate. She thought she was one of the luckiest girls in the world.

Yep. It was going to be a very, very good day!

Slight movement at the window caught her eye. A butterfly! No, three butterflies! The biggest, most elegant butterflies she'd ever seen! Her smile broadened as she whispered, "Thank You, Jesus! You know how I love butterflies." She watched, fascinated, as they settled gracefully on her windowsill. She'd never seen anything like them. If only she could reach her "Birds and Butterflies of North America" without scaring them off. She lay very still; trying to imprint their images on her mind... trying to figure out what was so strange about them...

Suddenly her quiet, serene world exploded. Giggles and shouts preceded little feet pounding up the stairs. Three-year-old EmmaLeah burst through the door, six-year-old E.J. so close behind that they both landed on their big sister at the same time. A small groan of regret escaped her lips... surely those breathtaking butterflies would be gone after all this commotion... Then she was inundated with chubby arms and legs and the sweet fragrance small children seem to exude in the morning, and she couldn't help but laugh.

She adored her little brother and sister. She had no doubt they were as much answers to her prayers as they were to her parents', and she treasured everything about them. She relished the panoply of Irish heritage the three of them displayed, each a vivid rendering of their ancestry. Her sister's curly red hair and blue eyes and their brother's chestnut brown eyes and white-blond hair were both so different from her own black hair and green eyes. But that difference had also troubled her heart more than she'd admitted to anyone—even herself. She watched them wrestling on her bed and her mind returned to the time she was forced to confront her sense of "differentness."

Not that she'd ever felt neglected. She knew how lucky she was to have a family that enjoyed each other so much. She hadn't even known why she often felt so out of place. She just knew her mom was gorgeous and she'd always wished she looked like her. Ellen Elizabeth O'Leary McConnell had the gleaming auburn hair and sky-blue eyes of romantic old movies like "Brigadoon." Elly hadn't much thought about it until her little sister was born, but one day she was watching Mom play "peek-a-boo" with Emmy and it hit her: They looked exactly alike!

She'd tried hard not to think, "Why her and not me," but there it was: same coloring, same tipped-up nose lightly sprinkled with the cutest freckles, same impossibly rosy cheeks, same delicate frame, same smile that lit up the room.

That's when THE question first whispered itself into her mind.

Then, when four-year-old Ethan James III began to replicate not just his father's name, but his burly frame and unruly straw-blond hair, the whispers became taunts... *So different from everyone else in the family!*

If only Eagan had lived, maybe he would have been the one to share her black hair and green eyes. If they'd had the chance to grow up together, maybe she'd have felt more comfortable in her own skin. It was probably strange to miss someone who died when she was only two, but he was her brother and sometimes she ached for him. She knew her mom did, too, even after all this time. She couldn't imagine how her parents must have felt when they lost their little boy. And then, after all those years... after all the prayers for another little brother or sister for her... after all the pain of accepting that it would be just the three of them... a miracle! And three years later, another!

But the whispers had just kept nagging at her heart. So, though she knew her family loved her dearly; that her doubts were illogical; in a moment of teen-age rebellion she'd finally shouted the question. Her cheeks flamed even now as she remembered how her anger had flung it at the one who loved her best on earth. Adopted?! She could still see Mom's face, shock almost immediately replaced by sympathy and then sadness. (Elly would have felt so much better if she'd just gotten mad.) She hadn't said a word—simply walked to the side table where she kept the family albums, opened an old one Elly couldn't remember noticing before, and gently laid it before her.

Her mind's eye still saw that old photo clearly. It could have been a picture of her in some sort of old-fashioned costume. "Who is *that*!"

"That, my dear first-*born* child, is your father's Great-Aunt Elly. Coleen Elizabeth O'Malley. You were named for her."

"But... but... I'm not named after you?"

"Sweetie, of course you are! You know how we Irish are about our traditions. You're the fifth generation 'Elizabeth' in my family, remember? But there were 'Elizabeth's' on your father's side, as well, and the moment you were born with Aunt Elly's black hair and porcelain skin, there was no question you had to be 'Elly,' too. I'm sorry I never thought to show you how much you look like Dad's family in the old country. I've always thought Aunt Elly was so beautiful, it never occurred to me it could be a problem for you."

One day soon Elly would research her father's family "in the old country." She was intrigued by this woman whose identity she shared and wanted to know more. But remembering the rest of that conversation still made her wince. Mom's tone had still been soft, but her eyes had taken on that warning look not even Dad ignored. "I think we need to talk about this adoption thing, though. I want you to think about this: What if you *were* adopted? Do you imagine we'd have loved you any less? If we'd decided to adopt a little brother for you after Eagan died, do you think he'd have been any less your brother? Or our son? Maybe we need to…"

A small hand softly twirled itself into her hair, drawing her back to the present. "Ooo, wook Sissy!"

She caught her breath. The butterflies were still there, sitting tranquilly in the window, wings outspread as if to bless the children with their beauty. Even E.J. grew quiet, watching them with big brown eyes. Elly pulled them both under her soft comforter, willing the moment to last. She wished her phone and camera weren't downstairs. If only she could get a picture of those three huge, never-before-seen butterflies. They'd been sitting perfectly still in her window for over twenty minutes now. It really was too strange! And stranger still, they seemed to be looking right into her room. A shiver touched her spine. Surely it was her imagination. Butterflies weren't capable of watching anything, were they?

"Kids, Gran and Pops are here."

The spell broken, her siblings raced down the stairs to welcome their grandparents. Elly grabbed her robe and took one last look at her windowsill.

The butterflies were gone.

7:30

She waited for all the hugs and "let-me-see-how-big-you-are's" and "I-wanna-sit-by-Gran's," and then the "bless-this-food," before she mentioned them.

"Mom, I just saw the strangest thing. Three huge…"

"Butterflies!"

"What?! How…?"

"Three absolutely huge butterflies are sitting on the window right behind you, Elly! I don't remember ever seeing any like them before. And if I didn't know better, I'd swear they were just sitting there watching us… Are you okay, Sweetie?"

Elly struggled to catch her breath, orange juice burning all the way down. This was too weird! There was no reason they should have followed her, even if they could have, but it had to be the same ones. Why in the world would they move from her upstairs window clear on the other side of the house to this one outside their kitchen? There was nothing on the window to draw them.

"That's what I started to tell you, Mom. They stayed on my windowsill for the longest time before we came down. And I thought the same thing—it was like they were actually watching us. It sort of gave me shivers, but I'm not sure why. You know how I love butterflies, but…"

Her voice faltered at the shadow that flickered across her mother's face, but in the next instant she thought she must have imagined it. Mom was laughing as usual, urging the little ones to "stop chattering and eat so we won't be late for church." Then they were all laughing at the children's excitement at their mother's promise that, "as soon as you finish, you can put on your new outfits for Elly's big day."

"Not just *Elly's* 'big day,'" she thought. It really was the biggest day of her life so far, but that was true for high school seniors across the area. So many towns were celebrating their graduation this afternoon. How many families were getting ready for their "big day" right now? And who could have asked for more perfect weather?

It was going to be a very, very, very good day!

8:00

Liz told herself she was definitely over-reacting. Why this sudden shadow of foreboding? Of course she had mixed feelings about her first-born child graduating from high school—any mother does. She knew this day would change their family dynamic forever. She knew it sounded cliché, but her daughter really was her best friend. She'd miss her terribly when she left for college in the fall, and though she knew it wasn't a conscious thing, she could already see Elly emotionally distancing from their safe, comfortable nest. But how could she complain? Bringing little fledglings to responsible adulthood was what parenting was all about, wasn't it? And their daughter was a fledgling to be proud of.

Certainly Elly had her moments, but most of the time Liz thought her namesake was almost too good to be true. Erin Elizabeth McConnell seemed completely untouched by the narcissism that plagued this twenty-first century. If anything, Liz worried she might be too much the opposite. She still felt badly that she'd been so clueless about her daughter's identity struggle. The possibility that Elly's stunning manifestation of O'Malley genes might actually lead her to question her place in their family had never entered her mind. But even that seemed just one of those battles of growing up—not a pre-occupation with self. The fact was this young woman who absolutely took one's breath away was utterly oblivious to her own beauty. If she noticed that eyes seemed to follow when she entered a room, she matter-of-factly assumed it was like that for everyone. If she thought at all about her academic successes, it was merely to be thankful she was rewarded for the hard work she was confident anyone could emulate. And that fierce love for God and family? Well, that was simply fundamental; she would countenance no suggestion it was exceptional. And though it was exceptional for an eighteen-year-old to care more about the young girls she mentored than her own social life, in Elly McConnell's eyes it was merely the logical response of extending to others the loving, supportive world into which she'd been lucky enough to be born.

Lizzy chuckled. Good grief! Talk about a doting mother! There was no way she could have voiced those thoughts without seeming like the sort of obnoxious parent she abhorred, even though every single one was true. Without question, the future of this exceptional young woman was… exceptional. But that was the problem, wasn't it. Liz wanted to believe she completely trusted God's promise of "hope and a future" for her little girl, but at times she couldn't help but wonder what that future might hold.

She was definitely over reacting! She'd always prided herself on refusing to play the protective mother. So why this compulsive desire to grab Elly and hold her close? Why this insistent feeling that something was wrong? It made no sense, especially today, when everything seemed about as close to perfect as life on this earth could be.

It was the butterflies! Ever since those magnificent creatures had settled at their window, wings outspread like some ethereal protector; she'd had this strange sense of impending danger. And, as so often happened, she knew Elly felt it, too. What was it she'd said? "It sort of gave her shivers…"

Unlike their Irish forebears, the O'Leary's disdained superstition. Growing up, Liz had sometimes thought her parents' zeal to debunk their Irish folklore had been a bit overdone. But as her own family grew, she recognized the wisdom of their warnings. A legacy of faeries and leprechauns and magical rainbows was intriguing, a fun tool to inspire a sense of unique heritage in their children, as long as it was kept in perspective. But mystic chains forged in ancient sacred groves are ever dangerous, and Elizabeth was grateful for her parents' commitment to the truth. She shuddered to think where her astonishing ability to sense the future might have led without their constant warning that her discernment was a gift from God, to be used for His purposes.

Today, though, that gift was leaving her troubled. She prayed it was just her over-active imagination. She prayed there would be no graduation tragedies this night… no graduation headlines to tear apart the heart of her community tomorrow.

With an effort, she pushed her premonitions aside and ran upstairs for a quick shower before time to get her "Little Mac's" dressed. Elly would want to show them off at graduation, and Liz was determined to give her daughter a very good day. A day to remember.

8:15

Ethan James McConnell II lounged in his favorite chair on their patio's wisteria-covered pergola, watching his two younger children run with abandon through the grass. He was tempted to join them. He couldn't remember a more beautiful day. Perfect for the graduation ceremonies that were scheduled around the area this afternoon.

He moved his chair so he could see them better. He didn't really need to; they were safe enough in their big brick-enclosed yard. He just wanted to bask in the moment; to enjoy watching them play without a care in the world. Though he never would have admitted it, even to Lizzy, the fierceness of his love for his children sometimes frightened him. He wondered if he'd ever quite get over the devastation of losing his first-born son. He wished eternity wasn't such a mystery. Oh, he didn't doubt for a moment he'd see Eagan again. He'd never have survived that terrible time without that assurance. But what would their reunion be like? Would they find the tiny baby they remembered? Was he a teen-ager right now, like his big sister, growing and learning? Or was he, as some writers theorized, transformed to his full potential the moment he reached heaven?

A gentle hand on his shoulder broke his reverie. "I think right now he's running in the greenest, most fragrant grass we could ever imagine, probably playing a game of stickball with your mom and dad."

How did she do that! She always seemed to know when he was longing for Eagan. Always seemed to know just what to say. He wondered if he'd ever been half as comforting to her.

"C'mon, kids. It's time to get dressed for church."

He tried to hide his smile at the predictable, "Please Mommy. Just a few minutes more? Pule-e-e-ze?" before he turned a stern face to say, "Go." He really couldn't blame them. He decided he'd stay here a few minutes longer himself. It was just such a perfect... What in the...

Two of those huge butterflies were perched on the wall, right above where the kids had been playing! He had to admit it was a little un-nerving to suddenly see them there, like sentinels assigned to guard them. He'd been amused at Liz and Elly's assertions that there was something "strange" about them; but now as he watched them basking there, outspread wings translucent in the sunlight, he conceded they were unlike anything he'd ever seen.

Ethan shook himself out of his musings. He'd better go see if he could help Lizzy get their little bundles of energy ready to go. He didn't know if it was the butterfly mystery, or the fact that her little girl was almost all grown up, or something else entirely, but beneath her cheerful demeanor he sensed an uncharacteristic tension, and he determined to do whatever he could to make this day as special for his wife as it was for their daughter.

9:00

Michael Patrick O'Leary thought something didn't feel quite right. When they had driven down from northern Missouri this morning, the weather couldn't have been more beautiful—even for the middle of May—and the forecast was exactly what families all over the area had hoped for. But years of farming had conditioned him to sense impending storms with almost the same instinct as the animals on his beloved ranch, and something just didn't seem quite right. Thoughts of the ranch brought a sigh. Might as well face it, he still really missed it. The decision to sell had been hard, but he was a practical man. When the doctor warned it was the ranch or his heart, he really hadn't seen much reason to hang on, so he'd given his future to God, put the ranch on the market, and watched it snapped up with breath-taking speed. He was glad they'd kept a few acres and the old home place, though, and of course Curious Clara had stayed. He'd never had a cow with personality before and he wasn't about to lose her. And last week she'd rewarded them with the most beautiful calf he'd ever seen. You just couldn't out give God, could you!

He whispered a prayer of thanks that he'd been given a little more time. It was so good he and Beth could be here with this family they adored, looking forward to celebrating their first grandchild's graduation. He had no doubt there'd be other graduation celebrations in that exceptional young woman's life, but somehow this seemed the most precious. He hoped he'd be here to celebrate the others, too, and eventually their Little Mac's as well, but Big Mike O'Leary was a pragmatic man, and he intended to wring as much joy and thanksgiving as possible out of every moment of every hour of this day. Something didn't feel quite right, but he would choose to be grateful, and he would do everything in his power to make it a very good day for his family.

9:15

Mary Elizabeth McCray O'Leary watched her husband of more than fifty years laughingly "race" his two shrieking grandchildren upstairs with her usual sense of protective pride. How her big, gruff rancher always managed such tender authority and rapport with every child in his life she'd never quite figured out, but she loved watching him with their grandchildren, just as she had with their daughter. However, she'd learned long ago that any attempt to express such feelings would be gently but firmly rebuffed by this man whose practicality and pragmatism bracketed a value system deeply rooted in his treasured Bible. A smile tugged at Beth's lips as she thought of those pages covered with underlines and references and annotations, just restored and re-bound for the fifth time and undoubtedly the source of Big Mike's strength as they walked through those early years of hope deferred and shattered dreams surrendered.

After Liz was born they'd eagerly planned for more redheaded, blue-eyed daughters and a whole houseful of "little Mikes" to hunt and fish and farm with their father. In the beginning, they'd prayed a lot, cried a lot, even bargained a little, but when the answer was finally, undeniably "no," Big Mike had taken a deep breath, dried his own tears and then hers, and chosen: He would honor his God and devote himself to helping salvage the "unsalvageable." And he would take his girls along for the most joyful, challenging ride that life could offer. Big Mike's "big girl" was more than grateful that his "little girl" had inherited not only his gift of discernment, but his cheerful, indomitable spirit. Surely that smile that lights up the room could never have

10

survived the sudden death of her four-month-old son and years of praying for another child without that spirit. But as for the discernment, Beth knew there were times her daughter found it more burden than gift. She wondered if this was one of those times.

"OK, Mr. O, you're sensing it, too, aren't you? I'm not sure what 'it' is, but there's definitely something on your daughter's mind besides the normal mother-of-the-graduate stuff. I'm pretty sure I saw that old look in her eyes just for an instant when those strange butterflies showed up. And I think Elly noticed it, too. What do you think?"

Mike looked at his wife in surprise. "I'm sorry, Honey. Guess I've been so busy looking at my own 'it' I missed that signal. Just can't seem to shake the feeling we're headed for a pretty big storm, in spite of what the weather looks like right now. Are you going to talk to Lizzy about whatever's on her mind?"

"There's so much going on right now I thought I'd wait until tonight when we're cleaning up after the party. Maybe by then whatever 'it' is will have all blown over. Speaking of that, do you really think it's going to storm today?"

"Ugh, bad pun!" Big Mike grinned. "Sure hope I'm wrong, or at least that all the celebrations are over before it hits. No reason to say anything about it yet, though. I really want this to be a day they'll always remember."

9:30
Ft. Scott, KS
Wilson Home

Alison Marie Wilson couldn't help but be just a little wistful. She thought she'd adjusted pretty well to the move a year ago, thank you very much. But no question, moving sixty miles from home for her last year of high school had been a challenge. She really missed all her friends in Joplin—especially Elly.

She smiled, remembering the solemn "pinkie promise" to be "friends forever" that they'd made when they were little girls. They still occasionally repeated it, jokingly locking pinkie fingers in the time-honored pledge; but they'd long ago recognized there was something profound about their friendship that needed no outward declaration.

Radical differences in appearance and personality had only served to deepen their bond. Elly, always tall for her age, was slender and willowy. Her long black hair framed delicate porcelain features dominated by solemn emerald eyes. Ali's petite curves, dancing brown eyes and pale golden curls were a perfect contrast. The girls seemed to balance each other out almost perfectly. While Alison depended on Elly's common sense to keep her grounded, her merry, carefree nature unquestionably enriched her friend's thoughtful, introspective character. Appreciating their differences had helped each girl become comfortable in her own skin, but neither seemed particularly impressed with what beautiful young women they were becoming.

They'd already talked and texted several times this morning. Ali thought she was much more excited about this day than her friend, even though Elly had been chosen to give one of the graduation speeches for her school. Come to think of it, maybe that was the problem. Her BFF Elizabeth was so-o-o-o responsible! Ali thought she'd probably already practiced that speech several times this morning, not to mention dreaming it all night. She smiled and shook her head, suddenly overcome with affection for this girl who shared so much of her life. "OK, Al," she thought, "there's no time to re-do make-up before church, and the last thing you need is mascara streaks down your cheeks. Besides, you're gonna see all your friends this evening."

It had been decided months ago. The girls were saddened to discover their graduation ceremonies would be scheduled for the same day, but they'd agreed they'd take lots of videos and pictures to share later, and Ali would head straight for Joplin after the celebratory lunch her family was planning. There was no question her heart was still there, and besides, the McConnell's gave the best parties ever! No way was she going to miss this one!

"Alison!"

"'K, Mom. Coming."

She hurriedly checked one last time to be sure she had the gifts for Elly from her parents and G-Paw Ed in her suitcase, then lugged it down the stairs to begin the celebrations of her big day. Later, she would remember the enormous butterfly that had been stationed on the dead rosebush by the drive, right next to her car door… and wonder…

2

GATHERING CLOUDS
SUNDAY AFTERNOON, MAY 22, 2011

12:30
Joplin, MO

"Elly. You've hardly said a word since we left the church. Are you nervous about your speech? It certainly looked to me like you were more than ready."

Beth smiled as she thought of her granddaughter's speech, neatly spread out on her bed for one last quick run-through, filled with the same underlines and references and annotations that adorned her grandfather's Bible. Those two may not look a thing alike, but they were like two peas in a pod when it came to personality and character.

It had already been such a good day. Surely, since they no longer had the 24/7 pressure of the ranch, they'd be able to spend more Sundays here with the kids. There was just something sweet about bringing the whole family together in church, and then sitting around a table in one of their favorite restaurants afterward. This family certainly never lacked for conversation—or laughs. Not with Big Mike and Ethan in the room. How gratifying, Beth thought, that their daughter had chosen a man so much like her father. Of course, Liz always said Ethan James McConnell II had chosen Michael Patrick O'Leary as father and friend, and she'd just happened to be part of the package. Well, whoever had done the choosing, they'd better start choosing to plan for those Sundays together right away. Elly had looked so grown-up in her cap and gown with the gold honors sash this morning at church, but it had just happened too quickly. In August, their little "willowy-wisp" would be leaving for college... and their little grandson would be starting first grade!

Ethan James McConnell III was trying not to be sad. This was his big sister's big day, and he wanted it to be perfect. A very precocious six years old, he'd long understood the concepts of "now" and "future." He knew that in the not-too-distant future, he would be the one in the cap and gown, maybe getting to give a speech at his graduation; and just a few years later, his little sister would be all grown up and graduating. He hoped he'd be able to take care of her then, the way he did now. Mom and Dad kept telling him he was her brother, not her father; but he was her *big* brother, and big brothers are supposed to take care of the little kids, aren't they?

He still remembered the day they brought her home. (People always tried to tell him he didn't really remember what happened when he was three, but he knew he did.) He'd tried to be patient that day— Gran and Pops were always so much fun—but he couldn't help it. He'd just had to keep running to the window, watching for their car. And then they were there, and Mom brought that little baby wrapped in a fuzzy pink blanket right to him first—even before Gran or Pops got to hold her—and the minute he saw her tiny pink face he knew she would be his forever. He would be the one to protect her and show her things, just like his big sister did him, and he was glad!

He thought Elly was the best big sister ever, but sometimes he couldn't help but wish his big brother hadn't gone off to Heaven so soon. He knew Mom and Dad tried hard not to ever make him feel bad about Eagan, but sometimes late at night he heard Mom cry, and one time she'd told him she still missed Eagan a lot. Somehow, that had made him feel better because he did, too, even though he couldn't figure out how he could miss someone he never really knew.

Now, his best protector and teacher (besides Mom and Dad, of course) would be leaving soon to go far away to college. He'd been trying really hard to be excited and happy for her, but he actually just wanted to wrap himself around her legs like he did when he was little and beg, "Please, Sissy! Please don't go!" He thought somehow she must know, because lately she'd been taking both of them almost everywhere with her. Then a new thought struck him: Maybe, just maybe she was gonna miss them just as much. Then he caught Pops'

15

eye in the rear view mirror, and he knew. They were happy sad, too! Maybe this growing up wasn't always so much fun, after all. Maybe he'd try to stop being in such a hurry and just be glad there were butterflies like the ones that watched Emmy and him playing in the yard this morning. E.J. was a very mature six-year-old, but he was only six, after all, and it never occurred to him that there was anything strange at all about two huge butterflies watching over them as they played.

3:00
South Range Line Road

"Elly! What in the world are you doing?" Elly stood frozen in place, a look of shock in those huge green eyes. "What's wrong?"

"Mom... look... don't you see them?"

Liz gasped. She'd been so focused on her daughter's sudden change of demeanor, she hadn't noticed. "Their" butterflies—now surrounded by a cloud of companions every bit as huge and unusual—on every bush in the small entry garden to the restaurant they'd just exited.

As usual, they'd had such a good time at lunch. But this time there was a hint of nostalgia under the laughter and teasing... a sense of reluctance to step into the new paradigm that waited. Then practical Liz (she was, after all, her father's daughter) had finally taken charge.

"Okay, family. Time to move on. It's going to take some time to find a parking place and we want to get there in time to find seats together, so-o-o, onward and upward."

Good-natured groans rewarded her effort to refocus them. They teasingly called her "the cliché queen" and she did her best to live up to the label. They'd straggled slowly out of the restaurant, laughing and chatting, and now stood grouped around that little garden area, staring silently at those mysterious butterflies. Except for Big Mike. He stood motionless just outside the door, staring up into the sky with a look of concern.

"Dad? Are you OK?" Liz followed her father's gaze. Nothing there but a few more clouds, but over the years she'd learned to respect that look. Something was bothering him, and that bothered her.

"Huh? Oh, sorry. It's just that all day I've had this feeling… If Elly's still planning to go somewhere with her friends after graduation, would you humor me and ask her to keep her car radio on and watch the weather? I think that storm will probably hit here around 5:30 or so, and I really think it's going to be a pretty good one."

That brought a smile and a hug from his granddaughter. "OK, Big Pops. I promise I'll be very careful. I sure wouldn't ever argue with you about the weather, and I certainly don't intend to be late for my own party tonight."

4:30
Missouri Southern State University

"El-l-l-l-e-e-e!!"

Oops. Sure was a good thing Elly loved to show off her little siblings so much, because there they went. They'd been so excited to see their big sister "up there on that big stage like a movie star" when she rose to give her challenge and farewell to the Class of 2011, but their mother thought they couldn't have behaved better. Elly had been wise to take them aside and tell them what to expect—and what she expected of them. Liz shook her head appreciatively. She just hoped her daughter would be half as effective a mom as she was a big sister, but she couldn't be prouder of her than she was right now. What a great message of "future hope" she'd just delivered! Guess it really was time to turn loose of her little girl and trust…

Well, she'd better go collect her clan and get those obligatory pictures taken. Mom and Dad wanted to drop by and see their friend Tom at St. John's, Elly was anxious to go meet Ali, and Liz wanted to be sure she got pictures of her with everyone in the family before they all headed out. She and Mom had had a great time decorating yesterday, especially after Elly insisted she wanted to help, and the basement was ready. But there were still a million details to finish before everyone arrived at 7:00 this evening.

4:45
Starbucks Parking Lot

Elly could hardly wait. It would be so good to see Ali again. They'd been the closest of friends since first grade. Even after the Wilson family had moved just across the border into Kansas, they still spent weekends and overnights together as often as possible. They might be complete opposites, but they shared every joy and heartache and dream. There'd been no question Ali would be at Elly's party instead of her own school's activities, but they wanted a couple hours to celebrate before then, just the two of them at their favorite coffee shop.

She wasn't there when Elly pulled into the parking lot. She was always early, so when Elly's phone chirped her friend's ring, she wasn't surprised.

"I hope you don't have a flat tire somewhere out in Kansas—or worse!"

She was relieved to hear Ali's easy laugh. "No prob, El. Just decided Books-a-Million coffee shop would be better. It's quieter, and we can pick out the books we're buying each other for graduation."

One of the things the girls shared was a love of books. They also shared a birthday, and as they'd grown up, their favorite way of celebrating was to spend as long as they wished in some new bookstore one of them had found, browsing, chatting, reading, and ultimately choosing a book for each other. Elly couldn't think of anything she'd rather do until the party.

"Great! On my way!"

5:00
Books-a-Million

By the time she got to the other end of Range Line, the skies were darkening and the wind had begun to pick up. Elly stifled a sigh of disappointment. Pops *would* have to be right! It had been such a good day. Oh, well, she and Ali both loved a good thunderstorm, and a little rain was certainly not going to dampen the celebration at her house tonight. She wondered if she'd even said thanks to Mom for all the work and planning she'd invested in making this night special. She resolved to do that just as soon as she got home.

Good. There was Ali's car. Elly felt a warm rush of affection as she watched her friend, already engrossed in the bestsellers display inside the brightly lighted bookstore. Of course, there'd be other times they'd see each other this summer, but their time today just seemed very special somehow. Soon enough, they'd be in different colleges, miles apart. Elly wondered if, four years from now, they would still be such good friends. She couldn't imagine ever being as close to anyone else as she and Alison had been all these years, but college had a way of changing everything.

Suddenly, she laughed out loud. What a goofball! Ali had noticed her car and now stood pressed against the window, thumbs in both ears in the silly "donkey salute" they'd shared since first grade. Better get in before it started raining. That peppermint mocha latte was calling her name, and she knew exactly what book she was buying for her friend this time.

5:15
McConnell Home

Ethan was trying not to pace. Liz was busy with last-minute details in the basement and the Little's were so excited they couldn't decide if they wanted to be downstairs with her or upstairs watching for Elly and Ali. The girls were still somewhere enjoying their beloved coffee and books, and in spite of himself, he was beginning to worry. It was looking like Big Mike was right about the weather, as usual. Elly had promised to keep her radio on and she surely would have heard the weather warnings by now. But if she and Ali were in the coffee shop, and he was sure that was exactly where they were, they might not hear them, and they obviously had their phones on silent. Well, he couldn't just sit here. If that storm was going to be as bad as Big Mike thought, the girls needed to be here, where they'd be safe.

"Lizzy. I'm going to go get the girls before the storm gets worse. We'll be back soon. If Elly happens to call, tell them to head right home and then let me know. Your folks should be back from the hospital by the time we get home. Keep the TV or radio on, OK?"

Ethan looked uneasily at the sky as he backed out of the garage. It was getting so dark! He really hoped this storm front would move on out by time for the party. Their sentimental daughter was so excited about having one last celebration with her friends, and it would be a shame to have to call it off after all Lizzy's work.

Still nothing but her voicemail. "Elly. It's about 5:15. I want you and Ali to come on home as soon as you can. That storm is looking pretty threatening and I don't want you out on the road. Call or text as soon as you get this."

5:20

Starbucks

Well, they weren't at Starbucks. That meant they were probably at Books-a-Million, buying each other a book again. Hopefully by the time he got to the other end of Range Line, they'd be headed home, but he wasn't taking any chances. The clouds were looking like none he remembered ever seeing before, and the rain was getting really bad. He wanted those girls home now.

5:30

Books-a-Million

The girls started as a sudden gust of wind threw gravel against the store window.

"Omigosh, Ali! Look outside. It's pouring and it's black as night! Dad's gonna kill me! I promised Big Mike I'd watch the weather."

Great! All she could get was Dad's voicemail. "Dad, it's 5:31 and we're just leaving Books-a-Million. I'm sorry—I forgot I still had my phone on silent from this afternoon. We'll head straight home and meet you there. Tell Pops not to worry."

Ali was clearly uneasy as they checked out.

"Maybe we should wait here until it eases up a bit, Elly. I'm not real excited about getting out in that wind."

"Me, neither, Ali, but I promised Dad we'd come straight home. We'll pull over if it gets too bad, OK? We can pick your car up in the morning. Ready? Le-e-t's go-o-o-o!"

Drenched from head to toe, the friends sat in Elly's car, trying to catch their breath and debating whether to risk the drive home. Elly was trying one more time to reach her parents when suddenly the lights along Range Line went dark. That was going to make the drive home interesting! Negotiating that busy thoroughfare could be an adventure for an inexperienced driver, even when the lights were working. Trying to drive the five-mile stretch to her turnoff in complete darkness in this storm, with no traffic lights, was a little more challenge than she wanted.

Well, it didn't look like it was going to get any better, so they might as well head south. She glanced at her friend, clearly intimidated by the fury of the storm, and hesitated. Maybe she was right. Maybe they should just wait here. But her family would be so worried, especially since the cell phones weren't working. They'd just have to take it real slow... hopefully, the lights weren't off all the way...

5:35

The darkened Books-a-Million lot was nearly empty when Ethan pulled in. At least they'd been there. Ali's car was still parked at the front. The girls must have decided to ride together and pick it up later.

This storm was getting worse! For a moment he considered taking shelter in the concrete building until it blew over, but since the lights were out he wasn't even sure he could get in. Besides he couldn't rest until he knew the girls were home safe and sound, so he whispered a prayer for them—and himself—and decided he might as well head back south.

5:39

South Range Line and 20th Street

Elly didn't want to admit it to Ali, but she was getting scared. She was a pretty good driver, but the wind hitting their car broadside was making it almost impossible to keep in the road. Maybe she should have pulled into the little strip mall on the corner of 20th and Range Line. Maybe she should turn around and go back there; it looked like there were still some cars there, even though the building was dark. She wished someone with a little more experience was here to tell her what to do, but... OK, she decided it would be best to keep going. Maybe it would be a little more protected along 20th Street. At least the wind wouldn't hit them quite so directly.

5:40
East 20th Street

"Al! We're going to have to find a safe place to pull over. This rain is like trying to drive through a curtain—I can't see a thing!" At her friend's soft whimper, Elly patted her hand reassuringly. "It's OK. I'm pulling into the first driveway I find until it lets up a bit. I just hope Dad isn't out hunting us. I'm sure he's worried sick. I'm so sorry I didn't do what Big Mike asked. I just hope no one has to suffer for it!"

3

FIVE FORTY-ONE P.M.
SUNDAY, MAY 22, 2011

Duquesne Village

Ethan found himself struggling to keep his big SUV pointed into the wind. He'd hoped this route on 20th and Duquesne would get him past all the confusion on Range Line. He knew he was risking missing the girls, but there was just no telling where they might be, and now his priority was getting home. They might even be home by now, he told himself, and at least he could make sure Liz and the kids were OK.

Now the wind seemed to be coming from all directions at once. Dear God! It was! Debris was hitting the car from all sides. He felt it lift off the ground, then settle roughly onto the road. There! That alley! It was probably risky to pull in among those trees, but the concrete building there might give him enough shelter to make it through what undoubtedly was the second tornado of his life. He pulled as close to the building as he could, whispered a quiet prayer for Elly and the rest of the family, and curled himself into a tight ball on the floor.

East 20th Street

Both girls screamed as they felt the car lift from the ground. "Ali! Oh God! It's a tornado. Quick, get on the floor!"

"No-o-o! You're not supposed to be in a car! We need to get into the ditch!"

"Ali! No! Stay here. At least the car will give us a little protection. Ali? No! Al-l-e-e-e-e!!"

Elly watched in horror as her friend was torn from the open car door and disappeared. Then everything went black as the twister spun her car 'round and 'round and dropped it back to the pavement like a child tossing a toy aside.

McConnell Home

Lizzy gasped as the monstrous black wall of water began to envelop their yard. She was so glad she'd taken Ethan's advice and kept the weather radio handy—especially after the power went out. Bless her disciplined husband's heart for being so meticulous about their emergency supplies. Now she and her Little Mac's huddled in the corner of the basement, hearing the vague echo of storm sirens, praying the monster would pass them by. She pled silently for her family, scattered across town on this day of celebration, and tried to keep a cheery tone as she pulled the guest bed's mattress over them and said in her most theatrical voice, "Can't get us here, big bad troll!" E.J., always up for a good game, giggled and made himself as small as he could. But Emmy didn't even react. Strange, thought Liz, she didn't seem frightened... just... distracted...

"Move!"

Liz thought it must have been the radio until the deep voice said once again, this time with urgency, "Move! Under the stairs—quick!"

"What... Who...?"

She wasn't sure how she got herself and two children across the room so quickly, but suddenly she was wedged into the space under the stairs. She hadn't even had time to grab the mattress—only enough time to throw herself over her babies before the roaring freight train was upon them and her world went completely dark.

St. John's Hospital

Big Mike and Beth struggled down the stairs, half carrying their friend Tom, shepherding his wife before them. Poor Teona was obviously terrified, but doing an admirable job of holding it together. They'd all been so relieved when Tom's doctor had agreed that he should come to Joplin for his surgery last week. It had been much too complicated for the small hospital close to them, but Tom had been recovering remarkably well—until now! Mike hoped they weren't killing their friend trying to save him, but the nurses had ordered every patient who could be moved into the stairwells and down to the basement. Strange, he'd always thought of this huge concrete edifice where lives were saved every day as impregnable. Now, it appeared it might be as vulnerable to the devastating force bearing down upon them as everything around it.

Just one more floor to go. Mike hoped they kept a crash cart in the basement. From the crushing weight bearing down on his chest, he thought he was probably going to need it.

4

AFTER the STORM
SUNDAY EVENING, MAY 22, 2011

5:52
Duquesne Village

The silence was deafening! Ethan gingerly extricated himself from the floor of his SUV. If you'd told him half an hour ago he would fit into that small space he'd never have believed it, he thought wryly. He'd better see how bad things were. If it was anything like the roar that monster had made...

But maybe it wasn't as bad as it had sounded. After all, he was still alive, and part of that garage was still standing. Thank God he'd followed his instincts and pulled in here. Maybe, as so often happened in this part of the country, the tornado had skipped across a few buildings without doing too much damage. That seemed to be the case every few years, and mostly people just took these storms in stride.

He stood in the pouring rain, trying to absorb what he was seeing. A massive bolt of lightning revealed... nothing! Except for the small section of concrete wall next to his car, the whole area was leveled! Houses, businesses, trees—the whole village—all gone! The next bolt of lightning confirmed it. One could see for what seemed miles in all directions.

He shuddered in horror. People would need help! There had to be colossal death and injury in those shattered blocks. He was relieved the car would still run. He would come back as soon as he could, but first he had to find Elly and check on Liz and the little ones. He wondered how long the tornado had stayed on the ground. Surely it had lifted before it reached their house clear across town. Still, this tremendous urgency could not be denied. Thank God his phone was still in his pocket. It looked like there was no voice signal, but at least he could text.

elly where r u? plz let me no so can come get u.

liz r u and kids OK? going to find elly. 5:50

6:00
East 20ᵗʰ Street

Elly thought she must have slept through her alarm. She vaguely remembered hearing it chirp, but she must be having one of those dreams where you feel you're moving in slow motion. She hated those—they always left her with such a feeling of vulnerability—and she was having a hard time moving her hand toward her night stand…

Suddenly her eyes popped open in horror. Ali! She'd seen her best friend sucked out of the car—how long ago? How long had she been here, unconscious? She struggled to unfasten her seatbelt. Ouch! There had to be some major bruises and cuts there, but it didn't feel like anything was broken. Was that what kept her from being sucked out, too? Ali would laugh if it was. She constantly hassled Elly to "click it."

"Ali!" Her voice sounded unnaturally loud in the eerie silence. "Ali! Answer me! Where are you? Ali," she ended in a sob. "Oh, pleasepleaseplease be OK. Ali!"

What was that? A moan? She scrambled out of her ruined car, somewhere in the back of her mind amazed that she had survived such destruction.

"Ali! Where are you?"

"El-l-e-e-e-e, help me-e-e."

"Al! I'm here. Keep talking so I can find you."

"In the ditch. Something's on top of me. I can't move."

There! In the drainage ditch under that big piece of metal roofing! She'd never be able to get that moved by herself—especially with all the stuff on top of it!

Where was everyone?

"Hang on, Al. I'm going for help."

"No-o-o! Don't leave me, Elly. You have to get me out of here. The ditch is filling up. You can do it. You always figure out a way."

She was right! Debris had sealed the culvert. With this downpour, the ditch would be overflowing in no time, and Ali would drown!

"OK, Elly, think," she muttered to herself. "You have to move the concrete block and stuff before you could hope to move that big log, but how in the world..."

A soft giggle stopped her short.

"I know... talking to myself as usual, huh."

She was relieved to hear another faint giggle. Ali must not be too badly hurt. Now, if she could just get all this stuff off her...

Uh-h-h oof! There! One concrete block, who-knows-how-many pieces of whatever moved, one huge log to go. If only it was lying the other way. If she tried to roll it the length of that piece of metal, would she risk injuring her friend? She had no idea whether Ali was hurt. What might she find when she finally got that big thing moved? Well, she didn't need to go there now, and it wasn't going to move by itself, so...

"Al. I have to roll a big log off the metal on top of you. I'll take it one roll at a time, and you have to holler if it hurts. OK?"

"'K." Her voice sounded fainter each time. Elly had to get her free *now*!

"Here we go... oh!"

How did that happen! Well, that thing *was* huge. It must have rolled of its own weight once she got it moving, but it hardly seemed to touch the metal!

"Ali? You OK? Did that hurt you?"

"I couldn't even tell you moved it. Can you slide the metal over? I'm trying, but I'm getting sort of claustrophobic."

"I don't know. Maybe I can lift one side enough for you to slide out."

OK, now that was unbelievable! She'd barely moved that big panel when it seemed to just flip over! Maybe it was the wind...

"Ali! Come on. Grab my hand so I can help you out—oh, oh-h-h your arm! Oh Ali!"

"It's OK, El."

Elly tried not to react as her friend stoically straightened her mutilated arm and cradled it in her other hand. She must be in shock. Elly just had to get some help.

"Is the man OK, Elly?"

"The man? What man?"

"A big man pushed me into the ditch and jumped on top of me and pulled that tin over us. I know that's what saved my life. I hope he's alright."

"There's no one else around, Ali. Come on. We have to get you out of there and find help."

"Elizabeth."

She whirled, half expecting to see her father standing there. A thrill of fear ran through her. Who was this huge man? How did he know her name?

But Ali seemed to recognize him. "Oh, there you are! I'm so glad you're OK."

In spite of her fear, Elly found herself strangely reassured by the authority in this imposing man's face.

"You're going to be alright, Alison, but I need to get you where they can take care of your arm. Elly, you have to stay right here. Your father will be here in a few minutes and he's going to need you at home." With that, he effortlessly lifted Ali from the concrete ditch, gently laid her maimed arm across her body, and turned to leave.

"Wait! Please, what's your name?"

The man's stern countenance softened as he turned an inscrutable smile on her. "Why don't you just call me 'Big Michael.'"

"What! What do you mean? Is Big Mike OK? How did you know our names? Who *are* you?"

But he was gone; and her sudden isolation became a crushing fear in the darkness. Then, mercifully, the lights of a car appeared—surreal in that devastated landscape. She watched the big SUV wind cautiously through the rubble-covered street and stop, bathing her in its welcome glow. Then she was sobbing in her father's strong arms.

"Daddy! Oh, Daddy. It's so horrible! How did you find us? Daddy... Mom? The Little's?"

"I don't know, Baby. I haven't been able to reach your mom, but then I couldn't reach you, either. I think the cell towers must be out." He looked around. "Elly, where's Alison?" As hard as he tried, he knew his voice held a note of dread at what he might hear.

Elly clung to her father, struggling to make sense through frantic sobs. "I thought she was dead, Daddy! The wind pulled her out of the car and then picked it up and I blacked out. She said a huge man pushed her into the ditch and pulled a big piece of metal over them. She's convinced if it hadn't been for him, she would have died. At first I didn't see him, but I think he must have helped me get all that stuff off her. I don't see how I could have moved that big log by myself." A sudden thought stopped her cold. "Dad... if he was under that piece of metal with Ali, how did he get out without moving all the stuff on top of them?"

"She probably just imagined him in all this chaos, Honey. Is she OK? Where is she?" He was getting more concerned by the minute. Something just didn't seem to add up here.

Another sob caught at her throat. "She wanted to wait it out at the bookstore. If only I'd listened, she might not have been hurt." She shuddered. "Daddy, her arm is horrible! I've never seen anything like that! But she didn't imagine the man. I saw him, too. He picked her up out of the ditch and took her to get help, but I don't know where."

"Well, I'd feel better if I knew where he took her, but we'll just have to pray he gets her where she needs to be. We'll look for her tomorrow, and get you checked out. Looks like you just have a few cuts and bruises, but I want to be sure. Right now, we need to see if we can get through to the house and check on the rest of the family. It's pretty grim out there and I don't want you going into shock, so humor me and lay your head back and close your eyes. You can pray for the family while I drive. Come to think of it, you can pray for *me* while I drive. It's worse than trying to navigate through a mine field."

Elly smiled thinly at her dad's effort to divert her thoughts as he eased back into the road. Obediently, she closed her eyes, and noticed as she did that the ditch was already full and running over.

She pulled her arms close around her and tried to stop her body's uncontrollable shaking. She was beginning to wonder if maybe she *was* in shock. She tried to pray, but the images in her mind wouldn't stop. They just kept running behind her eyelids like an old movie: Clouds, black and menacing as she and her best friend left the bookstore. Rain and wind, violently lashing her car as they tried to get home. Ali, disappearing into the storm and somehow landing in the ditch, protected by that piece of metal she insisted the big man had pulled over them. And that big man. How had he known their names, and where her dad was? Was it just coincidence he'd called himself "Big Michael?" The way he'd smiled, it almost seemed he was enjoying a little private joke. And those huge, transparent wings… Her eyes popped open. Wings! Had she really seen a shadow of huge wings when he bent over Ali in the ditch? No! That was ridiculous. It was just some optical illusion; some trick of the wind and lightning. Or maybe she was hallucinating. Whatever, she found it strangely comforting to remember how gently he'd lifted Alison from that ditch and disappeared with her into the storm. Somehow, Elly knew her friend was safe in the arms of "Big Michael." She smiled again as she thought of the stories they'd have to share, and how often she was going to hear "I told you so" about "the click that saved her life."

6:30
McConnell Home

Liz smiled at the tiny hand patting her cheek. She loved waking up to her sweet babies, even when she wished she could stay in bed a little longer. She tried to shake off the fog of sleep. Why was she having such trouble bringing things into focus? Was there was something she should be doing? What day…?

"Mommy? Mommy, you hafa wake up. The man say we hafa get out."

"What? What man? Emmy? What are you…"

Oh God! The tornado! It was so dark. "Emma, where's E.J.?" If she could just find the flashlight… wait… yes! Amazingly, her cell phone was still in her hand. She'd just started to call Ethan when the

31

twister hit. And it was still working! She shined its meager light around their small refuge, blood running cold as she realized the place where she and the children had first taken shelter was completely buried in debris. Thank God for whatever had made her move. Strange, it had felt almost like a huge hand pushed them into this corner! It had to have been the wind... The light fell on her tiny daughter, sitting quietly on what was left of the bottom step, an eerily tranquil expression on her face.

But where was E.J.!? "Emma, do you know where your brother is? E.J.!! Ethan James!!! Where are you!!?" She had to be careful—she couldn't let Emmy hear the panic in her voice.

"Not here. Uhver took him."

The world spun around her. Please, God, no. Not another son! She couldn't bear to lose another son! Please, no! But she had to hold it together. It wouldn't help for this child to be more traumatized than she was already. She had to find a way to get them out of this wreckage.

"What do you mean, Sweetie? Who is 'the other'? Was someone else here while I was asleep?"

"Sh-h-h."

"Emma..."

A little finger pressed against her lips, reinforcing a whispered, "Sh-h-h, Mommy." Emma sat, still as stone, appearing to listen. Then a confident smile and a whispered, "'K."

"He say we hafa get out. You hafa push the beam off and get up, Mommy. I hafa help."

Liz was becoming more and more concerned about her little girl. Could she be in some sort of traumatic shock? Then she realized Emma was right. Something had fallen across her legs! And how did that word "beam" enter her three-year-old mind?

"Who says, Emma? Who are you talking to?"

The indignant, how-can-you-be-so-dense look on her three-year-old's face would have brought a smile and a gentle reproof in any other circumstance.

"Me burfwy guy, Mommy. He 'tecking us, see? He wight here!"

A shudder of fear ran through Lizzy as she saw a huge man, standing quietly beside her defenseless little girl. She frantically shoved at the beam across her legs. She had to get out of here. What if he tried to take Emma like "the other" had taken E.J.!?

"Careful, Elizabeth," a musical voice sang into the chaos. "Let me help you. We have to get you out of here now."

She watched numbly as he effortlessly lifted the beam and raised her to her feet.

"Oh!" There was no feeling in her legs! If he hadn't kept his arm around her she would have fallen. Paralyzed? She pushed the thought away. She'd deal with whatever damage had occurred later. Right now she had to make sure Emma was safe and find out what had happened to her son and the rest of the family.

She wasn't sure how Emmy's "butterfly guy" got them out of that ruined basement so quickly, but she suddenly found herself sitting on the curb, cradling her baby safely in her arms as her husband's battered SUV rolled slowly toward them, torturously navigating around piles of detritus and fallen trees and downed electrical lines.

Then he was beside her on the curb, holding her fiercely. "Lizzy! Oh thank God you're OK!"

"There's my sweet princess!" as his tiny daughter threw herself into his lap. Then, hesitantly, "Liz... E.J.?"

"Bubby OK, Daddy. Uhver say he take care uh him. You see me burfwy guy? Wuzn't he wings booful?"

Liz shrugged her own question to her husband's questioning look. "She's talking about the man who helped us out of the basement. But I don't remember his wings." Her giggle sounded hysterical, even to her own ears. She looked around and found herself mumbling distractedly, "I guess he left... I should have thanked him... maybe he knew about..." Her words ended in a gasp as she glimpsed a small form stumbling out of the cloud of dust and debris. Strange that there could be so much dust with all that rain. And when exactly had that downpour stopped?

"E.J.?!"

Ethan turned at his wife's hysteria-tinged cry. In the next second he was on his feet, pounding toward that shadowy little figure. And then they were all piled together with Liz on the curb, laughing and crying and kissing, questions tumbling one over the other. Where had he been! How did he get outside! Was he OK?

E.J. accepted their excitement and attention with his usual cheer. "My butterfly guy carried me. I wanted to fly with him some more, but he said I had to come back because you needed me here. Can I fly with him again sometime?"

A faint sob caught Liz's attention. Just outside that joyous circle stood Elly, struggling to control her tears.

"Sweetheart!" The endearment brought her grown-up little girl into her outstretched arms, sobbing out her pent-up terror and confusion and pain.

"It's alright, Sweetie! We're all together, and that's all that really matters."

"No!" Tears gave way again to overwhelming terror and pain. "Ali's really hurt and Big Mike and Gran are gone! They said on the car radio that St. John's is completely destroyed. That's where they were, and I saw…"

"Poppy got sick, but he 'K 'cause Grammy wif him." Emmy's calm voice was so matter-of-fact, none of them thought to question what she was saying.

Liz realized Emma had been "listening" again, and tried to keep her voice level. She didn't want to frighten this little girl who'd already been through so much.

"Where are Poppy and Grammy, Emma? What do you mean, he got sick?"

A deafening roar stopped all conversation as what was left of their house collapsed into the basement. Liz and Ethan looked at each other in dismay. A few more minutes and…

Then they were all laughing in spite of themselves at Princess EmmaLeah's triumphant proclamation.

"Me burfwy guy take care uv us!"

With E.J. clinging to his big sister and Emma in one arm, Ethan reached a hand down to help his wife up. "Well, come on family. If Big Mike was at the hospital and got sick, someone there should know something. We'll start there. Then we'll find a place for you all to stay. There are lots of people who need help this night, and I need to see what I can do."

He looked at his wife in surprise as she made no effort to take his hand.

"You'll have to pick me up, Ethan. I don't know how long that beam was on my legs, but I haven't gotten the feeling back yet, and I don't think I could walk to the car."

His face ashen, he gently stood Emma beside her big brother and shot a warning glance at Elly's involuntary gasp.

"OK, big man. You'll have to help your sisters while I help Mommy into the car. Let's get her someplace where they can look at her legs."

"No, Ethan. We have to find Mom and Dad first."

"We need to find out how much damage that beam did, Lizzy. If St. John's is as bad as we heard, Freeman will be over-run, so I'm taking you to McCune-Brooks. Elly can stay with the kids and while they're checking you out I'll look for your folks."

7:15
Carthage, MO
McCune-Brooks Hospital

The drive from their demolished house on the southwest edge of Joplin to the outskirts of Carthage was surprisingly easy. There was very little traffic going out of the city. But already they were seeing rescue and news vehicles of all sorts streaming toward Joplin along Bypass 249. It seemed the whole world was converging on this ravaged corner of Southwest Missouri, and Ethan longed to join them... to do something to help his friends and neighbors who were facing what was undoubtedly the worst disaster of their lifetimes.

His first priority, though, had to be his own family. Once he knew they were safe and cared for, he would be free to throw himself into the rescue and recovery efforts. Until then...

A wave of relief swept over him as the cheerful lights of McCune-Brooks Hospital came into view. Though it was busier than normal, the brightly lighted Emergency Entrance felt almost other worldly in its well-ordered efficiency.

"Controlled chaos," Ethan thought as they wheeled his wife into the ER. He was so glad he'd once again followed his instincts and come here. The radio station was doing an amazing job of keeping area residents updated, and as he'd feared, with St. John's completely out of commission, Freeman was already having to refer to other cities. Only an hour and a half since their world had been so savagely turned upside down, and this small hospital north of the disaster area was already teeming with tornado-ravaged bodies.

He was reassured by the quiet confidence of the team that met them at the Emergency Room door. They quickly and expertly transferred Liz from the SUV's front seat to a gurney where they could stabilize her body before they moved her into the building. He desperately hoped he hadn't done more damage when he'd picked her up, but since she'd been sitting up on the curb he'd thought it must be OK to set her in the seat. His heart ached as he thought of his wife calmly sitting there, knowing she couldn't walk, but making sure her family was safe first. And what a gift his Elly was. He knew she was so worried about Ali and Big Mike and wanted to be with her mom, but she'd taken charge of the Little's without even being asked and made a game of finding the coffee shop.

7:25

Ethan sat by his wife's gurney in the little exam room, numb with the shock of this "very good day" gone so horribly bad.

"Ethan?" It was a quiet, wistful appeal.

"What do you need, Babe? Are you hurting?"

"Just wanted to hear your voice. I feel so strange, and I have to admit I'm worried about Mom and Dad. I'm not hurting, though... Maybe it would be better if I was..." she added almost under her breath.

What could he say to that? What could he do but lean over and gently kiss his wife and tell her he loved her? "It's OK if you're scared,

Honey. I certainly am. But I promise we'll find your folks as soon as we get you settled."

They waited, quietly holding hands, drawing strength from each other and from prayers to a Father Who unquestionably heard not only theirs, but the thousands of others being offered up for Joplin, MO, that fearsome night.

8:00

Ethan stood outside the room where they'd waited the past half hour, longing to follow the gurney that carried his wife as it disappeared around the corner. Though it was a relief that it didn't take as long as he'd feared it might, it was hard to watch them wheel her away to be poked and probed and stuck and scanned without him there to hold her hand. Well, he couldn't just stand here. Better go check on Elly and the Little's.

8:05

He wondered why he'd never visited this beautiful little state-of-the-art hospital so near their home before. There was a sense of hopefulness and calm that infused every public venue even now, when the airy, inviting atrium was choked with dazed, distraught humanity. As he threaded his way toward the coffee shop, he glimpsed a familiar figure.

"Beth?"

At the sound of her name, Elizabeth turned from staring at the elegant rock waterfall that dominated the entrance, brave face slipping a bit as she saw her son-in-law coming toward her.

"Ethan! How did you find us? I've been texting and trying to call, but I never could get a signal. I'm so glad you're here. Are Liz and the kids OK? Was the house hit?

"Yeah, the house is gone, but everybody's here. Did your friend make it? Is Mike with him? Beth, stay with me!" He reached out to steady her as her face seemed to suddenly lose all color.

"Mike had a heart attack, Ethan. We were helping Tom and Teona down the stairs right before the tornado hit, and I guess the strain was just too much. St. John's is in complete ruin—it's unbelievable!

I'm amazed at how well everyone was handling all the confusion and suffering, though. I still can't imagine how they got us all up here where Mike and Tom could get help."

"How bad is he, Mom?" Ethan couldn't keep the pain out of his voice. He loved Big Mike and Elizabeth like his own mom and dad. They'd taken him under their wing, treated him like a son when his own parents had died in a horrible car crash when he was a teenager. If they hadn't been there to shepherd him through those dangerous years, his loneliness and anger could have sent him off the rails. He adored his wife, and of course she was more than "just part of the package," but there was more than a little truth to her claim that he'd fallen in love with her family first. He'd claimed them as his own long before he ever noticed the O'Leary's pesky little tomboy had become the prettiest girl in town. They all knew the doctors had warned that Mike's heart could be a problem, but Ethan wasn't ready to let his friend and mentor go.

"They don't know yet. They're still running tests, so I decided to see if I could find Teona and see how Tom is." Finally, the tears came. "I'm scared, Ethan. Mike's not afraid to die, but I'm afraid to think about living without him."

Ethan thought his own heart might die. He wondered if this might be the final blow that would undo him. How could he tell this woman who'd given him so much that he'd failed her when she was already in such pain? That her daughter might never walk again because he hadn't been there to protect her when she needed him most? Logic was telling him that was irrational... that he couldn't be responsible for something over which he had no control... but logic had no place in that over-crowded, beleaguered hospital while the monster that had changed so many lives forever was still smashing its way through the Four States.

"Beth, I don't want to tell you this, but..."

Her eyes widened as she focused on his anguished face.

"Oh, no! Who? Oh, Ethan! I've just been so absorbed in myself I didn't even stop... Who... please, not one of the children?"

"It's Liz, Mom. A beam fell across her legs and right now she has no feeling in them... Here, we'd better sit down before someone has to pick us both up." In spite of his best effort, his voice broke. "They just sent her for an MRI; hopefully we'll know more soon." He knew a tearful, shaky son was not what she needed right now, but it was the best he could offer.

He wasn't really surprised when suddenly this woman who faced losing the ones she loved most dried her tears, squared her shoulders, and took charge. He'd seen her do it before. His quiet, fragile-looking mother-in-law somehow had an amazing ability to reach into some hidden store of courage and become the one on whom everyone else could lean in crisis.

"Poor Elly! She must be terrified. Are she and the babies here? We need to go find them."

"I sent them to the coffee shop. You know Elly. She'll keep the kids entertained, but I know she needs some encouragement. She's pretty blown away about her mother, and she's been so worried about her grandfather." To Beth's questioning look he simply said, "She can tell you the whole story."

8:10
Coffee Shop

"Gra-a-a-m-m-m-e-e-e!!!" Worried, exhausted people packing that little coffee shop shared a grateful smile at the tiny girl's exuberance as she raced into her grandmother's arms, older brother trying hard to maintain his six-year-old dignity as he followed. "Grammy, our burfwies came back and they wuz so-o-o big. They saved Mommy an' E.J. an' me..."

"Sh-h-h, Emmy!" E.J. was looking uneasily around the crowded room. "We can tell Gran about the butterfly guys when we get home." Every face was turned toward them now, some with what seemed more than just polite curiosity.

But Elly was looking anxiously past her grandmother. "Gran?" Her voice held a breathless, pleading quality. "Where's Pops?"

Beth felt an overwhelming urge to protect her younger grandchildren from any more fear and trauma. "Here, Daddy, why don't you take this $5 bill I found in my pocket and see if you can find some ice cream for my two favorite butterfly spotters while Elly and I catch up on all that's been happening."

He knew she was right. Their two Little Mac's had had enough turmoil to last a lifetime, but Elly had already been alone too much in the midst of all this heartbreak. She was trying valiantly to hide her panic, but those black-fringed eyes always gave her away. He was reluctant to leave her again, even in the hands of a grandmother who loved her more than life itself. Well, it was hard to accept, but if he didn't trust these women he treasured to Hands much bigger than his right now he wasn't going to make it through this night of horror. He drew a ragged breath and struggled to steady his weary voice.

"C'mon guys. Grammy's treat. All we have to do is figure out where to find ice cream in this hospital in the middle of the night." A warm little hand in each of his, he couldn't resist one last glance back, just to reassure himself. That was strange. He'd never thought those two looked alike before. Maybe it was that determined set of the jaw...

Sheer determination kept green eyes brimming with tears from spilling over. "Gran? Please... Pops...?"

Equal determination kept Beth's soft voice steady. "They're running tests right now, Sweetheart. He was trying to get Tom down the stairs to safety at St. John's and they're sure he had a heart attack. They just don't know yet how bad it is." Her granddaughter's sharp intake of breath brought an arm around her shoulder. "He'd do it again without hesitating, Elly. It's just who he is..." Then, head to head, they allowed the tears to flow. Big Michael Patrick O'Leary was such a larger-than-life force in this family. They couldn't begin to contemplate what it would be like without him.

Elly was the first to stir. "Gran... Remember our butterflies this morning? A huge man helped Ali and me, and I could swear at one point I saw enormous wings that looked just like one of them. I'm sure it was just a trick of my mind, but the Little's are so confident they each had their own "butterfly guy," and Mom said some big guy just appeared in the basement and got them out right before the house fell. I keep feeling like this is some weird dream we're all going to laugh about in the morning."

Beth's eyes had a faraway look as she responded. "I have a feeling we'll be hearing many 'weird dream' stories before this is all over. Here. Dry your eyes and blow your nose and walk with me up to CCU. Let's check on our own big guy and see if they've found him a room."

8:30
Mike O'Leary's Room

Big Mike woke to find Beth and Elly quietly standing beside his bed, hand in hand. "Either I'm in heaven and two angels are bending over me, or that's my gorgeous wife and granddaughter I'm seeing." His voice was husky around the oxygen cannula. "Where's Lizzy? All my girls OK? Ethan and E.J.?"

That was Michael Patrick O'Leary. A practical man. Right to the heart of things. And one had better not try to evade his questions.

Beth took a quick breath and obediently dove in: "The house is gone. The kids are OK, but Lizzy was trapped under a beam and her legs were injured. Ethan's strong as usual, but he's hurting; just waiting to hear from the doctor. We'll let you know what we find out as soon as he gets to see him. Your doctor says your heart is going to take time and rehab, but it could have been a lot worse. I haven't seen Teona, so I don't know anything about Tom yet, but they're saying you saved him by getting him out of that room. Now, your wife needs to go check on your son-in-law, and your favorite granddaughter needs a bear hug. You're gonna love some of the stories she has to tell you."

Coffee Shop

Ethan sat at the small table in the coffee shop, willing himself to be patient… to treasure this quiet moment watching his little ones enjoy their treat. He. Would. Not. Drum. Or pat. Or look at his watch…

B-z-z-z. He was impressed with the technology and efficiency of this small hospital. Assigning a text number for a cell phone was so much better than trying to communicate over a PA system one could never understand. Well, Beth and Elly were still with Mike, so hopefully the staff would be so busy they wouldn't notice ice cream drips or sticky fingers. He couldn't just sit here when they were looking for him, and he wasn't about to deny these children the one good thing they'd been given this night.

He looked up in surprise at the man and woman who slid chairs over to join them.

"Unca Fwank!" The slight man's surprisingly deep laugh boomed as Emmy launched herself into his lap and patted his bald spot with those sticky fingers. Frank and Ginny Zimmerman led the church home group that met at the McConnell's every other Thursday. In Emma's eyes, Ginny would do in a pinch, but "Unca Fwank" was her personal property. When she was just a tiny thing, he'd won her over by requiring a kiss "right there" before she could sit on his lap, and now it was ritual. Occasionally he allowed himself the wistful dream of a beautiful red-headed bride kissing him "right there" for luck before she took her father's arm for that walk down the aisle, but two rounds of chemo had reduced his slight frame to almost skeletal proportions, and recently some of those little indiscernible signs of another recurrence had been intruding on that dream. After all this time, he was nothing if not pragmatic. If that dream ever became reality, it would be only by God's grace.

"Do you have someone here? Are you...?" They'd been through so much the past few years; Ethan hoped there wasn't more bad news. At least their home here on the outskirts of Carthage would have been untouched by that monster storm... unless...

"It's really bad, Ethan. The church is setting up a task force to locate all our people, and they already have a prayer line set up. They've designated the building as a refuge for now. We heard you were right in the path, so we thought we'd better track you down. How badly were you hit? Is anyone hurt?"

Ethan wasn't sure whether the presence of his friends gave him strength, or permission to fall apart; but right now he *had* to hold it together, so all he could manage was, "Lizzy. They're running tests and just texted me. Could you..."

Ginny stopped him with a pat on his arm. "Go! We need some time with our favorite buddies anyway. Let us know as soon as you can. Ethan… Elly? Your folks?"

"Mike's in CCU—Elly's with Beth," he shot over his shoulder as he gratefully ran for the elevator. He knew they'd be praying, even as they entertained his Little's, and that gave him strength.

8:35
Patient Consulting

"There are no fractures that we could find, Mr. McConnell. That's reassuring. It's too soon to tell how much nerve damage there is, if any. About all we can do for now is watch her a few days and see what happens. Just a word of encouragement—the body is designed with a wonderful capacity to repair itself, even when we 'experts' have no idea what to do. She's sleeping. The nurses will tell you which room."

He offered his hand and hurriedly started to move away; then turned a tired "Yes?" to Ethan's, "Doctor?"

"Your job has never been harder than tonight. We'll pray for you."

Eyes that were trained to project impersonal, confident compassion were, for a fleeting moment, vulnerable and heavy with the weight of overwhelming need. He nodded curtly, then turned and was gone.

9:00
Liz McConnell's Room

At first Lizzy was terrified. The huge man stood there again, unmoving, an aura of immense power surrounding him. Then she saw his face, and peace transcended her terror. She wanted to say, "Thank you so much!" She wanted to tell him how much his help meant to her family. How awed she felt in his presence. But she couldn't seem to swim out of that dark warmth. Maybe didn't really even want to…

"Lizzy. Sweetheart." She turned away in annoyance at the interruption. She remembered that voice—thought she probably should do something to relieve the note of anxiety in it. But this was such a beautiful, comforting place. She thought she might just stay…

"Lizzy! Elizabeth! Honey, you have to wake up! We need you!"

She sighed; reluctantly opened her eyes, and watched the man she'd adored since she was eight years old come slowly into focus. Were those tears on his cheeks? Oh no! The kids? No, they were all safe. Dad! Oh no! Not dad!

"Ethan?" They were both surprised at how weak her voice was. "Did you find Mom and Dad?"

"They're here. Your mom and Elly are with Big Mike in CCU. Don't panic. He's alive, and apparently saved the Andersons' lives. Hopefully your mom has had a chance to talk to the doctor by now. I'm headed up there in a few minutes and I promise I'll let you know what I find out as soon as I can. So, how's my girl? Need anything? Are you hurting?"

"I was sleeping so hard, I have no idea what I need yet. You know, Ethan, it's a strange thing, but right before you came I was dreaming that I woke up and that huge man who got me out of the basement was standing here. At first I was terrified—he seemed to exude such power—but then he looked at me and I just felt such peace wash over me. I can't explain it, but I'm not afraid anymore."

"Well, as usual, I'd better be willing to learn from my wife," Ethan smiled as he moved a side chair closer to the bed and took her hand.

"Ethan, you need to go check on Elly and the folks. I'll be OK."

"Shh, don't talk. I will soon, but right now I need some time with my best friend. I'm getting there, but I still just get petrified when I think how close I came to losing you. Let me sit here while you go back to sleep and then I'll send Elly down in an hour or so."

10:00

Lizzy woke to find that sometime while she slept, the big hand holding hers had been replaced by the slender, delicate hand of her daughter. Elly sat, head back against that hard chair, sound asleep. Lizzy lay there, watching dreams play behind her daughter's eyelids, wishing she could pick her up and put her in bed with her, the way she had when she was little.

"Elly-bug." It was only a whisper, but instantly Elly was alert, ready to care for her mom. Lizzy wordlessly held out her arms, and care-*giver* became care-*needer*, sobbing in her mother's arms.

"Oh, Mom. I thought today was going to be such a wonderful day... I'm sorry..."

"It's OK, Sweetie. Sometimes tears are the best thing to help us cope. I'm afraid there'll be many more before this is all over. But I've been lying here thinking how much we already have to be thankful for... How's Pops?"

Elly laughed through her tears. "Telling everyone what to do, as usual. Gran got to talk to the doctor, and he says a few days in the hospital with some meds and then *faithful* rehab should get him back on track again. In fact, he said this may have been a blessing in disguise because it's a warning to... H-m-m... OK, point taken."

"Mom, you know how some big guy showed up and got you and the Little's out of the basement? Well, it's really bizarre, but Ali says some huge guy shoved her into the ditch and pulled a big piece of metal roofing over her when it hit. From all the stuff on top of it, there's no question that's what saved her. I didn't see him right away, but I'm sure he helped me get everything off her so we could get her out." Elly shuddered, and the tears began again as she remembered her best friend calmly rearranging her mangled arm. "Oh, Mom! Her arm looked like something out of a horror movie! I don't ever want to see anything like that again! But suddenly that big guy was just there, telling me she'd be OK and scooping her up like she was a kitten or something. I still can't quite sort it all out. He knew our names, and he knew Dad was coming. And what really terrified me was, when I asked his name he said, 'just call me Big Michael,' like it was some sort of joke. For a minute I was afraid Big Mike was... Then, when he bent down to pick Ali up, I could have sworn I saw..." She took a deep breath and plunged on, "Mom, he had huge wings that looked just like one of our butterflies this morning! How can that be! I feel like that tornado blew me into some other universe and somebody's going to tell me to follow the yellow brick road any minute now."

Her mother said nothing, just waited until she was ready to go on.

Suddenly she brightened. "She's here, Mom! I got to see Ali! Somehow that guy got her here really fast and she was one of the first ones they worked on. Her arm was absolutely shattered and she was in surgery several hours, but there just happened..." She caught her breath and paused thoughtfully, "...*just happened* to be an orthopedic expert visiting here from Houston and he was able to put everything back together. They think she'll get full use of her arm back, and she's having a good time telling everyone about her mysterious superman." She paused, a cloud again covering the momentary cheer. "I love her so much, Mom, and I feel so guilty! She wanted to stay at the bookstore, and I insisted on trying to get home. Why couldn't I have been the one..."

"Elly, I'm sure there'll be a lot of 'what ifs' and 'if onlys' because of everything that's happened. Don't waste energy you're going to need to get through it on 'whys.' You made the best decision you knew at a frightening moment. I'm sure Ali knows that, and God knows what He's doing. Just watch what He brings out of all this in the next few weeks and months. And don't try to *be* Him."

"Ouch." Elly grinned and hugged her mom gently. "Just for that, I'm gonna go tell Gran you're awake. She's dying to see you."

11:00

Ethan stood lost in thought, staring vacantly out the window, torn by conflicting needs and priorities. He was so grateful his family was safe. Even with all the questions about Lizzy's future, he knew how blessed they were. How much worse it might have been. His heart ached for all the families who weren't all together this night of tragedy and loss. And he longed to *do* something, anything, to try to relieve some of the suffering.

"It's OK, Ethan.

"Hm-m-m? What? I'm sorry, Honey, what did you say?"

Liz had watched her husband staring out at the lighted, tree-garlanded parking lot the last few minutes and knew he saw nothing but the demons troubling his mind. She knew him so well. Knew exactly what he was thinking. God hadn't somehow used a flimsy concrete wall to protect that lone SUV in the midst of complete devastation so its driver could rest comfortably in a safe, lighted hospital while only-He-knew-how-many were still trapped and suffering in darkness. Their family was safe. Others needed his help.

"You can't just sit here when people need help, and I can't sleep when I know you're troubled. Mom and Dad are OK. The Little's are probably sound asleep at the Zimmerman's. Elly's busy playing courier and encourager. And I need rest. To be honest, it terrifies me to think of you out there in the middle of who-knows-what, but I know you. Let Elly and the folks know what you're doing and please try to at least text when you can. And Ethan, please be safe. I expect you to be here when I wake up in the morning."

Ethan didn't trust his voice. He stood a moment gazing at his wife; then tenderly pulled the covers over her shoulders, kissed her on the forehead, and was gone.

11:05
CCU Waiting Room

"No!"

"Please, Dad. Surely you, of all people, know I can't stand to just do nothing."

"Elly, I saw things just driving across town that I don't want you to remember the rest of your life. And I won't be much use if I'm constantly worried about you. Besides, you *are* doing a lot. I don't think you realize how much you've helped keep everybody's spirits up and pulled together as a family. Tell you what; they're going to need help at the church tomorrow. Frank said they're already over-run with donations and people needing help. When I get back in the morning I'll take you over and you can help there. I imagine your mom's already asleep, but you can check in on her after you give your grandmother a little break. Then, I want you to find a place you can get some rest or you're not going anywhere tomorrow.

11:15
Bypass 249

As Ethan eased into the stream of vehicles flooding into the city, he could hardly believe the difference from just a few hours before. How could so many have come so quickly! Now there were not only rescue and news crews, but law enforcement and military convoys; huge dump trucks and heavy equipment and personal vehicles of every description; and even farm tractors pulling flatbed trailers and digging equipment. How many on this road had simply dropped everything to go where people were in need? His aching spirit was touched by the outpouring of concern and his heart went out to many who would be haunted for life by what they were about to experience. Just his drive across town right after the tornado had seared into his mind things he'd hoped never to have to see again. And yet he went. He could not turn away when so many were trapped and injured and dying.

Surprisingly, traffic flowed quickly and efficiently along the highway. It seemed every vehicle moved with one accord. The urgency of their mission was palpable, infusing every driver with a generosity of spirit not often seen on the nation's roads. Then, every heart sank as debris began to appear along the ditches several miles from town. They would discover later that medical records and family pictures and pieces of everyday lives would be found as far as seventy miles away.

Though the queue had poured smoothly into town without difficulty, near the disaster zone it slowed to a crawl and then stopped, moving inch by inch into utter devastation. Checkpoints were already set up. National Guard, State Patrol, first responders and sheriff's officers from across the region were evident at every shattered intersection.

Now, Ethan thought, where could he be the most help? If things were as bad at St. John's as he was hearing, that was probably the place to begin. He was sure they could use the supplies and blankets the McCune-Brooks people had sent.

Dear God! He'd thought he was prepared, but this was like trying to drive through a war zone! He had no idea how he'd found his house a few hours ago. In this dark chaos he had no clue which street he was on. Every landmark on which he'd depended without even thinking about it was just gone! Wait... there was St. John's... what was left of it! He was surprised by the bile rising in his throat. His head was literally spinning. For a moment, he thought he would be sick. It was a miracle anyone had survived such destruction, and his mom and dad had been right in the middle of it!

He joined the column of vehicles at the roadblock. Minivans, pickups, SUV's, tractors with trailers, anything that might be used to transport injured people waited in line. Frantic workers dug through piles of rubble, furiously trying to reach those who were still trapped. Others stood in dazed confusion or wandered in shock. Suddenly he pulled out of line into a side street. Thank God for those blankets! He quickly wrapped one around the partially-clothed woman who'd just stumbled out of the dark carrying a bleeding child and eased her into the front seat. She stared at him mutely, eyes vacant with the horror of it all. She clung desperately to that poor little mutilated body, and he didn't waste time trying to examine it. Somehow, he had to get close enough to Freeman Hospital to get help. At least it looked like their generators were working.

It was absolutely mind boggling! This city's state-of-the-art medical district had been savagely cut in half! From 32nd Street north, all that was left of the extensive, beautifully landscaped St. John's complex were the windowless, shattered shell of Joplin's largest hospital and piles of rubble where homes, nursing homes, clinics, doctors' offices, pharmacies, and other medical facilities had been. From that key thoroughfare south, Freeman Hospital with its ancillary medical complex stood completely untouched. The fire fighter guarding that checkpoint took one look at the specter in Ethan's front seat and waved him urgently through.

7:00 a.m.
Monday, May 23, 2011

Ethan was surprised by the dawn. He was beyond exhausted. He'd completely lost track of how many bleeding, broken bodies he'd transported; how many trips to hospitals and triage areas his once-beautiful SUV had made; how many times he'd stopped to search... rescue... comfort... even reunite frightened pets with grateful owners. He didn't even know what time it was. His heart yearned to do more; to go back one more time; to help sift through the heart-breaking scenes the rising sun was revealing; to try to bring hope to one more suffering neighbor in his hometown. But his car was out of gas, and, he had to admit, so was his body. And now that he'd taken time to catch his breath, he realized how much he needed to be with his loved ones; this time not as their protector, but as a wearied, wounded, haunted man.

He allowed his battered car to roll slowly into McCune-Brooks' parking lot and sat, trying to collect his emotions. Cheerful morning sunlight reflecting off the pristine windows of this little hospital just a few miles from such suffering and sorrow seemed almost obscene. But it was where his aching heart could be comforted; where he could gain strength to face the nightmare once again.

He exited the car slowly, like a man weighed down by the burden of too many years, hardly able to stay on his feet. He was much too fragile to face his injured wife yet. She needed him whole, so he slipped quietly into his father-in-law's tranquil room. Big Mike was alone, sleeping peacefully. Ethan carefully slid a chair close to his bed, laid his throbbing head on the big man's shoulder, and sobbed.

He went to sleep then, soothed by rough farmer's hands gently stroking his hair, just as they had a broken-hearted orphan boy named Ethan so many years before.

5

BUTTERFLY PEOPLE and OTHER MIRACLES

3:30 p.m.
Tuesday, May 24, 2011

The death count now stood at 116. Missouri's governor had been in Joplin for a first-hand look at the damage. At a news conference he'd announced that 265 National Guard and 110 State Troopers had been assigned to help in rescue and recovery as well as control traffic and looting; and federal assistance had been promised. Though rebuilding help would come later, the Governor noted, first the missing must be found, and the region's culture of faith-based involvement and neighbors helping neighbors was a vital factor in the search.

"I just ask that everyone throughout the region, throughout the country, continue to pray for folks as we work out there," he said. "There are other people out there that could be surviving and we need to make sure we're in a very organized way going about the search as these leaders—very organized leaders—are doing right now."

4:30 p.m.
Joplin, MO
College Heights Christian Church

Elly was bone tired. Even her toenails hurt! But she was so glad Dad had agreed to let her help here at the church again today. She wasn't sure she could have survived just hanging around the hospital or the Zimmerman's; and besides, all the churches in town that were still standing were overrun with clothes and supplies and volunteers and people coming for assistance, and they needed all the help they could get. She was proud of her church, though. As soon as the tornado struck, they'd closed out all their school's activities for the year and opened their doors as a shelter; and refugees and donations began pouring in. Cases of bottled water filled one of the parking lots. Eighteen wheelers lined up, awaiting volunteers to begin unloading donations. Now, only the second day since that monster storm had totally destroyed a third of their town, every inch of every hallway and classroom and meeting space in this huge, sprawling building was crammed with every imaginable material need—even children's toys and books and games—and it all had to be sorted and categorized and cataloged and made available to the still-uncounted families who'd lost their homes and belongings. The church had almost immediately been designated as a primary distribution center, and its leaders had responded with typical vision by bringing in a professional disaster response group to help them get organized and train volunteer workers.

She glanced through the registration sheets covering the sign-in counter where she'd been helping. She'd once heard someone say that the worst of times brings out the best in people, and these sheets seemed to prove it. Volunteers were pouring in from all over the country. Groups from churches and businesses and charitable organizations—and just concerned individuals—were dropping whatever responsibilities they had in their everyday lives and coming by caravan and bus and private car, bringing with them tools and equipment and donations, staying in area hotels and private homes and even campgrounds, and making themselves available for whatever needed to be done.

Suddenly a volunteer coordinator's voice rang through the building: "Shut everything down! We have to get everyone out of here by 5:00! The weather forecasters are saying another bad system is heading right for us, probably be here by about 6:00, and we want everyone home and in shelter before then."

"Please, no, not another one!" The plea was unspoken, but Elly saw it repeated in the sudden quiet tension around her. She darted a glance out the big plate glass doors. The sun was still shining, but those clouds were getting dark, just like... just like that bright Sunday afternoon that had turned so deadly. She shuddered. How could they survive another one like that? But she absolutely refused to give in to panic. Surely whatever crew Dad was working with would have been warned and he'd be here before it got bad. She tried to keep her hands from shaking as she grabbed her phone.

"Elly, wrap up whatever you're doing right now and let's head for Carthage. Your Mom will be worried sick if she hears there's another storm coming and we're out on the road."

She whirled at the sound of her father's voice, surprised at the urgency in it, and at the strange comfort she felt that he shared her alarm. She thought that people all over this fractured community were probably feeling the same dread. Stories were already being told of people who hadn't taken the warnings seriously until it was too late. She'd be willing to bet no one ignored the warnings this time.

Uh oh! That girl she'd just been talking to was planning to stay at a campground! She couldn't be much older than Elly herself. She still couldn't believe that delicate-looking young woman had driven all the way across the state by herself, equipped only with a pup tent and a cooler and barely enough money to pay for fuel. What was her name? Amanda. They had to find her. Dad wouldn't consider letting a young girl like that stay outside alone—especially on a night like this—any more than Elly would. She could certainly throw her sleeping bag on the floor of Elly's little room in her safe new basement home for the next few days.

6:30 p.m.
Carthage, MO
Zimmerman Safe Room

After all she'd seen of God's care for them, Elly felt guilty about being so scared, but she just couldn't help it. Memories of terrifying winds and unimaginable destruction and complete helplessness were still too fresh.

She'd felt so bad for Dad. She knew he was torn, trying to figure out how to protect all his family when they were so scattered, and though she'd urged him to be with Mom and the Grand's at the hospital, it had been harder than she'd expected to see him drive away in that increasingly battered SUV. Now she and her new friend huddled with her little brother and sister and the Zimmerman's in their basement shelter, praying that the storm raging outside would stay "just" a thunderstorm. She pictured her splintered house, briefly allowing herself to mourn the rain and wind's final destruction of her "stuff," until she became aware of discussions around her.

The neighbors who lived on either side of her hosts had gratefully crowded into the little safe room, uneasily joking that "all this togetherness was one way to get to know each other better." Then, like every gathering in this storm-battered region, the conversation turned to storm story miracles; some of which were making the circuit, some they actually knew first-hand:

> *A neighbor's aunt impulsively moves her two children from their bathtub refuge into a closet at the last minute, and emerges to find it is the only part of the structure left standing.*

> *A child's pet bunny is found hopping among the ruins of their home, freed unharmed from its smashed cage that was somehow deposited on a shelf high on the one remaining wall while her baby chicks' cage is blown under the house, still intact, every chick alive.*

> *A friend's small son escapes the wreckage of his home to get help for his mother and sisters and shouts, "Don't flick the lighter, there's a broken gas line!" Then later matter-of-factly explains, "God told me to warn her, of course."*

> *A group of friends take shelter in a public park bathroom. As the storm bears down, two big men stand against the walls and literally keep them from falling in, but when the group turns to thank the men, they're nowhere to be found.*

> *A colleague's wife is alone in their basement when she feels something push her into a corner seconds before a huge bookcase is blown across the room, forming the only shelter where she could have survived.*

A mother pulls into the Home Depot parking lot to find shelter for her two children and is horrified to see a car hurtling straight for their windshield. She throws herself over them, bracing for the worst. But, nothing happens! As she tells friends she can't imagine how it could have missed them, her little boy calmly announces, "The butterfly people held onto it so it couldn't hit us."

A little girl calmly rides out the storm in the basement with her grandmother and later tells her mother she was not afraid because the butterfly people said they would "keep it quiet for her." She describes them as "really big and white and all wet." The mother thinks she was trying to describe "shiny."

A couple tries to take shelter in Dillon's Supermarket but can't get the door open. As the twister hits they dive under a nearby SUV and when it is over, find a large piece of metal has wrapped around the car, creating a cocoon of protection around them.

Suddenly all conversation stopped as E.J.'s "big brother" voice impatiently rang out above the echoing thunder, "I already told you three times, Emmy! My butterfly guy said they'll still be taking care of us, even if we can't see 'em. But he said we won't see 'em when we don't need 'em."

Emma idolized her big brother. She seldom believed he could be wrong. But this time… Well, she had a butterfly guy, too! Big blue eyes glared down at chubby fingers weaving a dance of frustration. Little chin quivering; she said adamantly, "Di'n't tell me-e-e!"

Frank moved quickly to comfort his "little princess," pulling her onto his lap and whispering in her ear. After a moment of surprise—after all she always had to kiss him "right there" before she could sit on his lap—she inclined her head close to him, listening intently. A frown and shake of red curls, more intense silence, a little face slowly brightening, then a nod and a reluctant smile.

Ginny caught her husband's eye and nodded imperceptibly toward E.J., sitting dejectedly in the corner. He'd just been trying to tell his little sister the truth. Why was Uncle Frank acting like he'd done something wrong?

"Emmy, would you like to tell your brother what we talked about?" Another frown and slow shake of the head. She wasn't quite ready to forgive E.J. yet.

"May I tell him, then? I think it would make him feel better. I know you love your brother, and right now I think he's feeling a little sad."

For the first time, Emmy looked up. Suddenly she slipped off Frank's lap and ran to wrap her arms around her brother. "Don't be sad, Bubby! Unca Fwank say you just tryin' uh take care uh me. Me jus' mad 'cuz you got to talk to you burfwy and me di'n't. Sowwy."

E.J. patted his sister, looking gratefully at Frank; then glanced around the crowded room in embarrassment.

"E.J." Stuart, the man who lived west of the Zimmerman's, sounded almost wistful, "can you tell us what your butterfly guy looked like?"

Frank, ever ready to protect his charges, relaxed at the sincerity of the question.

E.J. shot a silent "help" at Uncle Frank. At six he was old enough to know that some people would not believe what he and Emmy had seen, and he never liked being the center of attention.

But this was Emma's chance to shine. Maybe her "burfwy guy" wasn't talking to her anymore, but she could talk about him. She stood in the center of the room; arms stretched wide, blue eyes sparkling with excitement. "So-o-o big! Gweat big wings, so booful! An' when he talk it make me happy an' 'cared. He tell Mommy get unner steps an' then he put he wings over us. Wind so woud me got weally 'cared, so he make it quiet for me. After uhver take E.J., he talk to me 'till Mommy wake up so me won't be 'cared. Mommy cuddn' move the beam, so he move it and pick us up and take us out uhva basemen'. Then Daddy come an' E.J. come back inna cwoud. Mommy an' Daddy an' Sissy waffed and cwied, but me didn't 'cuz me burfwy already tole me uhver wuz bringin' him back." For a moment that "cwoud" seemed to have settled over her sunny little face. "Bubby got ta fwy wif he burfwy. Wush..." She brightened again, "...but me burfwy say he pwoud me stay an' take care uh Mommy."

At Emma's declaration that her brother had gotten to fly with his "butterfly," all eyes turned to E.J. He didn't say a word, just solemnly nodded his head.

Stuart's wife Marg said softly, "We've been hearing stories of children saying they saw 'butterfly people,' but it's been a little hard to believe they weren't just stories. Now we're looking at two who really saw them..."

"Three," said another voice resolutely.

If any mind had questioned the little McConnell's stories, all were steadfastly fixed on the bigger McConnell as she took a deep breath and quietly began recounting the story of Ali's rescue. She confessed her terror as she saw her best friend torn out of the car. Her voice caught as she told of her relief at hearing Ali's voice under that big piece of metal roofing. She talked about her dismay at the huge log that pinned her beneath it and then her shock at the almost supernatural ease with which it moved. She shared her horror at the sight of her friend, calmly straightening her mangled arm, and her apprehension when a huge man appeared, not only knowing their names, but where her father was. She hesitated, then plunged on to describe "Big Michael"... his frightening aura of power... his tenderness as he bent to lift Ali from the ditch... his huge, translucent wings...

She stopped then, spent from a long day filled with hurting people and the anxiety of another deadly storm, but even more from the trauma of reliving those moments in the midst of an EF5 tornado. She sat, lost in thought, until she became aware of total silence in the room. Well, it was the truth, and she needed to tell it, whether they believed her or not. But she dreaded to look at Amanda. What must she be thinking! Slowly she raised her eyes and saw her new friend staring at her, tears streaming down her cheeks.

"Oh Elly. Thank you so much for bringing me home with you tonight. I came to Joplin because I just had to do *something*, and I guess I didn't think things through very well about trying to stay in a pup tent. I can't imagine being out there right now by myself..." she shuddered, then went on, "...but I have to admit since I saw the stories on the internet about little kids seeing 'butterfly people,' I've been dying to know more. I prayed all the way here I could talk to just one. Now I actually *know* three! I'm so thankful I came."

Now burly, tattooed Hector moved to offer an approving pat on the shoulder. Twenty-four hours after the storm of the century had torn so many lives apart, eight adults and two children had crowded into a safe room designed for four, fearful of another night of terror, grateful for a place of refuge, but uncomfortable to be so close with virtual strangers. Ninety minutes later, ten friends, ages three to sixty-three, shared one reality: Their stories were part of a plan much bigger than themselves. No one even noticed that the storm had passed.

6

The VICTORY of SURRENDER

5:30 a.m.
Wednesday, May 25, 2011
McCune-Brooks Hospital

Lizzy was depressed. She might as well admit it. The harder she tried to deny it, the more depressed she got. She'd been keeping her spirits up pretty well, so how come she woke this morning feeling so down? Had she somehow assumed if she could just be cheerful enough and think of everyone but herself, she'd wake up some morning with legs magically working again? She certainly knew she was one of the lucky ones. Some of the stories she was hearing made her want to hide under the covers and never come out. People were dealing with realities more hideous than any horror movie ever conceived. But she was so helpless, and her family needed her. She'd always been the one who held them all together…

"Don't try to be God!" The reproof seemed almost audible. What was it Mom used to say, "Choose your words carefully—someday you may have to eat them?" OK, it had seemed so obvious when she'd warned Elly about it, but what did "trying to be God" look like right now? Was she supposed to just suck it up and get over herself? Or…

"Hey, how's my best girl today?"

The forced cheer in that tired voice she loved so much melted her heart. Before she could stop them, the words tumbled out. "I'm afraid that girl disappeared sometime during the night. The one this morning's pretty discouraged."

The relief that washed over her husband's face stopped the apology on her lips cold. "Thanks for being honest with me, Sweetheart! I was starting to get a little worried that you were trying so hard to be strong, you wouldn't give yourself a chance to heal."

That opened the floodgates. "It's just so frustrating, Honey! You're working from sunup to sundown, rescuing and searching and salvaging. Elly's at the church, helping people try to put a little of their lives back together. Mom's all over the hospital—she's already got a whole notebook full of prayer requests. And all I can do is lie here. Someone else is even taking care of my babies. Not that I'm not terrifically grateful for all the help, but it's just... s-so... h-hard..." The intensity of her sobs shocked her. It was the first time she'd cried since the tornado, and she wrapped herself in the sheltering arms of her husband, sobbing until she could sob no more. She never noticed that her tears had unleashed his own. And neither of them noticed the older version of herself, standing just outside her door, sharing their tears of pain.

9:00 a.m.

Ethan and Elly had been gone an hour or so when her mother appeared at the door, two nurses and wheelchair in tow. "Hey lazy girl. It's time to get out of that bed and go cheer your father up. He's about to go nuts—they'll only let him up to go to the bathroom and to sit in a chair a few times a day—and the doctor thinks you're going to get your strength back sooner if you're up some."

She didn't know which was stronger, the fear of trying or the exhilaration of finally getting up and out, but there wasn't a moment to contemplate it before the nurses expertly slid her out of the bed and into the waiting chair, then acceded to her mother's unspoken demand that they allow her to "drive." As she knew her mother intended, it was a turning point. Her spirits were restored, especially when they'd wheeled her down to the coffee shop to have "McDoggles" with her Little Mac's.

Emma had clung to her mother, sitting ever so still on her "wap" so she wouldn't "hurt Mommy's sore wegs." Lizzy had seen her nurse react, but she didn't care. She couldn't see how legs so completely dead could be any more damaged, and holding her little princess and smoothing back her little big man's mop of hair was the best therapy she could think of. Apparently the nurse had decided the same thing, and had resignedly bitten back warnings of more injury. Now back in her room she rested; exhausted, but completely at peace that God was in control of whatever the future held.

2:00 p.m.
East 26th Street Disaster Zone

"OK, people. We have to call it a day. It's just too dangerous to stay here in this storm. We're hearing someone was just struck by lightning, so please pick up your tools and find your van."

If Ethan could have gotten past his own frustration, his heart would have gone out to his crew supervisor. These volunteer leaders worked alongside their crews all day and then spent several more hours at the church each evening assessing and laying out strategies for the next. He knew their determination to find every still-missing person only intensified as the rains continued and each day grew harder. The volunteers they supervised were more than willing to keep working, rain or no rain. Having to stop now had to be even more frustrating for them.

He stared out the van window as it slowly cruised their block, picking up workers waiting at curbs still piled high with debris.

"Why, Lord!" Suddenly, the seeming futility of their efforts consumed him. "There are still too many lost! Maybe we could still save some, but every day it rains those stinking piles of rubble just get more dangerous! Wasn't the tornado enough? I just don't understand. WHY DON'T YOU STOP THIS RAIN?!"

Furtively, he glanced around the bus, certain they'd all heard that embarrassing outburst. But everyone there seemed lost in their own weary thoughts, and Ethan was left to wrestle silently with his God. That overpowering anger was surprising... and frightening. From where had it come? How could he justify such rage at a Father who'd shown him and his family so much undeserved mercy? Was he actually angry about other families he couldn't help, or helplessness at his own family's pain? Lizzy's tears this morning had been a relief. He knew it was a healthy thing for her to stop trying so hard to keep a brave face. But he had to admit he was so glad she hadn't noticed how those tears had absolutely undone him; that no one had been there to see him fall apart. He just had to stay strong. His family needed his protection and reassurance.

5:00 a.m.
Thursday, May 26, 2011
McCune-Brooks Hospital

"Oh! Ouch ouch ohhh! Elly, help! Rub my foot! Oh!!" Liz found herself sitting up in bed, jolted by agonizing pain.

Elly was immediately wide awake in her bedside chair, heart racing. "Mom! What's the matter? Do I need to call for help?"

Her mother forced a laugh. "No. I'm alright. It's just my foot. It's cramping so hard it's killing me! Oh! Please! Rub it!"

Elly scrambled to massage the ache away, then stopped, staring at her mother with wide eyes. "Mom? Your foot's cramping?"

Liz stared back, a huge smile spreading across her face in spite of the pain. Pain! "Elly! My foot's cramping! IT'S HURTING!"

"MOM, YOUR FOOT'S HURTING!"

By now both women were laughing and crying, bouncing up and down on the bed like school girls. Medical staff suddenly crowded the room, ready for whatever emergency must be unfolding. Julie, who had cared for Lizzy since the tornado, got it first. "Mrs. McConnell! Your foot is *hurting*? Let me see…" Quickly she threw back the corner of the sheet to reveal five pink toes, drawn into an obvious but gratifyingly normal cramp. Practiced fingers worked muscles and tendons, and Liz sighed with relief as the cramp released. Careful to keep her professional face from slipping, the nurse exposed the other foot. Warm and pink!

Sharp-pointed surgical scissors in hand, she instructed, "Close your eyes and tell me if you feel anything." Tip of her finger lightly probing the top of Liz's foot, she queried, "This?"

"I—I think so. It feels kind of fuzzy…"

Now not quite touching: "Now?"

"No-o-o." Liz struggled not to sound disappointed.

Now the sharp point gently probed the big toe, and before she could ask, "Ouch!" Now the bottom of the foot. Now the heel. Then the same routine with the other foot. All brought joyful expressions of pain.

All attempts at detachment forgotten, Julie turned excitedly to call the doctor and slammed into Ethan, still panting from his sprint down the hall. Hearing the disturbance in his wife's room, he'd arrived breathless and fearing the worst. They all laughed as fear turned to confusion and then joy at the news that Lizzy's foot was… hurting!

By evening, sensation was slowly, excruciatingly returning to both legs. It seemed that each nerve awakened in turn, determined to make itself known before conceding to the next. The family met in the cafeteria to celebrate. Even Big Mike had been allowed the trip down, portable oxygen tank a point of great fascination for his grandchildren who were still shepherded by Frank and Ginny. Then Elly arrived, pushing Alison and followed by the Wilson's in triumphal procession; and their interest quickly turned to the "awesome" cast on Ali's arm, held rigid by a metal frame around her waist. Like almost every meeting place in this anguished region, complete strangers related as family, and there were smiles on almost every face as the children solemnly, carefully wrote their names on it and then claimed bragging rights as best.

The celebration was short. Lizzy, apologetically exhausted at all the examining and testing, had nonetheless resumed her role as commander-in-chief and firmly declared she and Big Mike and Ali had had enough excitement for their first day out. As they headed back to their rooms, she couldn't help but think that though their joy at being together again had been almost tangible, even that was tinged with the melancholy of pain and suffering that had invaded their quiet community. There was still so much loss yet to face, so many hurdles yet to cross, so much grieving yet to do.

8:00 p.m.
Saturday, May 28, 2011
East 20th Street Disaster Zone

Ethan sat on the littered curb, heedless of the filth and rubble all around. Six days since the monster came roaring through his town, and it seemed they'd made little progress against the mountains of wreckage and debris. How many of his neighbors were still missing and unaccounted for? How many might be still trapped and alive? How many had been recovered today, giving their anxious families at least some degree of closure? How many of his co-laborers dreaded each shovelful as he did, wondering what they might uncover?

Each morning when he reported to the church for his assignment, he was humbled and amazed at the hundreds waiting to sign in to be given their instructions and equipment and join the swarms of volunteers spreading out across the city.

One day dissolved into the next, surreal in its chaos and confusion. He couldn't remember ever being so weary. Actually, he couldn't really remember ever feeling rested. Was it only a week ago his family had joyfully looked forward to a day of celebration? Had their world really been neat and ordered and predictable and safe? He guessed most people at their core understood there was nothing truly safe or predictable in a fallen world, but seldom were they confronted with the brutal reality of today.

A white pickup cruised slowly through the neighborhood, workers in the back offering bottled water and snacks to the many who, like him, still tried to eke out a few more minutes before darkness called a halt to their work. It had become almost an obsession. They were driven by one thing: to conquer the death and destruction left by the monster that had attacked their homes and families.

He was finding it harder and harder to decompress at the end of each day. He was glad tomorrow was Sunday. He couldn't remember a time he'd needed more desperately the hope and healing his church family would offer, but it was going to be hard to walk into that service without Lizzy. The church was so much a part of their life together. Of course she'd insisted he take the children, and of course he'd comply. They needed as much normalcy as they could give them in this upside-down world.

It would be painful to walk in without her, but it would be even harder for her. Being confined to a hospital bed instead of there with her family was especially egregious for someone like Liz, but until the doctor thought it was safe for her to leave the hospital, it just wasn't worth the risk.

Well, here was his crew leader, and though his spirit rebelled at quitting while there was a moment of light and an ounce of energy left in him, he certainly had no desire to make that difficult job harder, so he gathered his tools and was obediently waiting at the curb when the van came by.

7

HOME IS...

10:00 a.m.
Tuesday, May 31, 2011
McCune Brooks Hospital

Lizzy sat in the room that had been home for nearly nine days, surprised at her reluctance to leave it. On second thought, why should she be surprised? It was the only "home" she had at the moment... a sobering thought... one she'd been able to keep at bay until now. She tried to remind herself there was so much for which to be thankful.

Frank and Ginny had proven to be the kind of friends for which one could only hope. It made her time here in the hospital so much easier to know her Little Mac's were being cared for with such love and dedication. She couldn't help but smile at the memory of those two quiet, frail-looking people expertly shepherding two little bundles of energy through the hospital's still-crowded lobby Sunday night. The family had gathered in the cafeteria once again; this time to celebrate Ali's release. How gratifying to think of her at home in Kansas now, determined her last summer before college would not be ruined by "any old broken arm." She and Elly had already slipped back into their habit of texting or talking several times a day, and Lizzy had a feeling their little blond friend would start college in the fall with a degree of maturity and hard-earned confidence most of her peers lacked.

They'd all celebrated when Big Mike was pronounced well enough to transfer to his regular doctor at home. Even Tom had recovered enough to travel back to Northern Missouri. Liz tried to find comfort in knowing her parents' decision to go back yesterday confirmed how well she was doing, but she knew the veiled look of sadness in their eyes when they had come to say goodbye had only reflected her own. It was hard to see them go; even harder for them to leave before she was out of the hospital. If they could have, they'd have stayed until the family was settled into a new home, but Big Mike was a practical man. His heart still needed healing and therapy—it would do no good if he pushed himself into another heart attack and caused the family even more pain—and with 7,000 homes gone and volunteers from all over the country flooding the area, there was absolutely no place to stay. It was a great relief to all of them that Frank and Ginny's basement apartment could easily accommodate Ethan and Liz and the kids as long as they needed it, but there was certainly not room to house two more adults. Besides, though their new neighbors had been great to take care of things for them, Dad had confided with the old twinkle in his eye, he was anxious to see how Curious Clara was doing with her new calf.

Though the Little's had seemed to be doing well under the Zimmerman's care, she still got misty eyed when she thought of the moment a few evenings ago when E.J. had asked if he could "help her walk." He'd conspiratorially steered her to a deserted corner of the waiting room and confided he'd been missing home so much it made him cry. Something in his eyes had told her there was more, so she'd just waited as he'd squared his little shoulders and continued. His "butterfly guy" had visited "one last time" and told him not to be sad, that someday they'd have a house he'd like even better than the old one. "B.G." (of course her practical, systematic son had named him) promised that even if E.J. couldn't see him he'd always be there taking care of him, but right now E.J. needed to be a big man and help take care of his family 'til his mom was well. So, her little big man told her solemnly, she didn't need to worry about his sisters. He'd make sure they were always OK, and he'd help Frank and Ginny, too. And when she got home, he'd get her anything she needed. All she'd been able to do was hug him tight, so proud of her little guy, so sad he was having to grow up so fast.

"Ready, Babe?" She was touched by the note of excitement in her husband's voice. "You're all dismissed, finally, and the escort is bringing your wheels... you OK?" So much for her game face! He could read her like a book.

"I was just thinking about the kids and all they've lost—and trying to be thankful for all we *haven't* lost. It's weird, Honey. I've been so looking forward to getting us all back together, and now, well, I think I'm a little scared." She tried to smile. "Guess I've just gotten spoiled, being waited on hand and foot."

"Not weird at all, Lizzy. I know 'being waited on hand and foot' has been hard for you, and it's still going to be awhile before you're back to normal. Just remember everyone else has had more chance to get used to a new reality than you have, so please cut yourself some slack. I warn you, the world out there is a pretty scary place right now. There's not much left of the Joplin you remember and seeing the neighborhood in such ruin is going to be hard." He smiled at the young escort who appeared at the door with a wheelchair. "Now Madame," he said with a flourish, "your chariot awaits, and your kids are fit to be tied, so quit foolin' around. Let's go!"

10:30 a.m.
Range Line Road

In spite of Ethan's attempts to warn her, it hit with brutal force. Until about 13th and Range Line, everything seemed pretty normal. Just another day in this quiet little town in the middle of fly-over country. Then they topped the hill and confronted the unimaginable. Everywhere, huge piles of rubble covered the ground and lined the roads and dotted the landscape. Crumpled, smashed vehicles rested where they had dropped, often several deep. Twisted, broken skeletons were all that remained of lush trees that once shaded these comfortable neighborhoods. Streets were no longer recognizable, stripped of all identification, and she yearned for familiar landmarks. Her stomach knotted as she realized *everything* was leveled as far as she could see in every direction. How many schools and churches and businesses and homes were simply no more? How many died or were horribly injured along these once-thriving avenues, now crowded with massive trucks laden with scrap metal and debris and pieces of her neighbors' lives? She'd never seen so much traffic in her small city. Every neighborhood was a beehive of volunteers and work teams and heavy equipment and relief centers.

Crushing bands of sorrow wrapped around her heart and tightened with each devastated block. Instinctively she wrapped her arms around herself, rocking back and forth, unable to restrain the wracking sighs that seized her, deeper and heavier with each agonizing breath. She wondered how she could survive this ride through Hell. She wondered if this suffocating pain would ever go away.

But then, in the midst of it all, her God showed up. She saw Him in the crosses that never fell, standing strong even as the church or hospital or school they represented was reduced to rubble around them. She heard His compassion in marquees that implored "pray for our community." That defiantly proclaimed concern for each other... and faith in tomorrow... and appreciation for the help that came streaming through their city's wounded thoroughfares. As they passed the crumbling shell of the high school, she felt His encouragement in its battered "Joplin High" sign transformed to "HopE High" by resourceful students with duct tape; and in the school's mascot eagle surrounding it, carved from broken tree trunks by local artisans confidently declaring His promise of renewal. She knew He must be smiling at the spirit and humor of spray-painted signs on shattered buildings: "Yard sale, everything must go; Teardown ready; Loot 'n I'll shoot; We're OK, we will prevail; Down not out; I'm safe, we will pray; Survivor, we will rebuild; God is here; God bless everyone." And everywhere one looked were smiley faces and "God bless Joplin."

Then she saw the flags, and pain gave way to pride in her community! On every ruined street, from every improbable standard, Old Glory echoed "God Bless America." Adorning fences and equipment and passing vehicles, painted on shattered walls and crumbling stones, standing resolutely in piles of debris, flying proudly from broken houses and twisted branches, lining streets by the hundreds on miniature poles; everywhere she looked the Red-White-and-Blue fluttered in the morning sun. (Where did they find all those flags amid such confusion?!) In the worst of the ground zero area, a tattered flag hung boldly from the highest remaining branch of a twisted, leafless tree. Another, respectfully at half-staff, waved serenely in front of the wrecked Academy Sports building. And now, as they drew closer to home, a huge, pristine one covered at least two stories of the ravaged face of St. John's Hospital, momentarily soothing her trepidation at confronting their loss for the first time in the light of day.

11:00 a.m.
McConnell Property

At first, she wasn't even sure it was the right place. Everything in this battered landscape seemed alien. As they drove slowly up the barren street, she felt... nothing! She didn't know exactly what she'd expected, but it wasn't this! Her logical mind argued this was where they'd lived, but her heart insisted, "No!" Their street had been filled with echoes of parties and backyard barbeques and shared triumphs and tears. It was where they'd joyfully brought four babies home to great celebration, and sorrowfully said farewell to one who would not grow up there. Reason reminded her she'd been right here on this curb when what had been left of their house collapsed, but grief contended this shattered pile of rubble could not possibly be where they'd settled and become family and raised their children. Where was the flower-filled yard where their little ones had watched for Daddy to come home and chased fireflies with neighborhood friends and played games until dark? This littered, broken concrete where they parked could not be where three children had learned to ride big wheels... and two had graduated to bicycles... and one had graduated to the family car; where, with a mixture of pride and dread, they'd watched their firstborn child back ever so carefully out and into the world of independence—could it? If she closed her eyes, Liz could still see their inviting, tree-lined drive where, like a slideshow playing across her mind, a four-year-old Elly happily drew pictures with big colored chalk from her Easter basket and then a grown-up Elly nostalgically helped her little brother and sister do the same. She watched a six-year-old Elly, long black hair flying, skate determinedly around that circle drive; and later, black tresses next to the blond ones of her best friend, spend hours sitting on the curb, chattering and giggling as only ten-year-old girls can. She could still feel the bark of the mammoth tree E.J. always chose as "home base" in countless games of hide and seek... still smell the fragrance of the huge old rosebush that had stood at the corner of the house, where Princess EmmaLeah had reigned at her little table and chairs, insisting Daddy have "one more cup of tea" before he went to work.

Liz reluctantly opened her eyes, took a deep breath, and opened the car door.

"Honey, are you sure you're strong enough..." Her husband's protest died in his throat as she said tonelessly, "I have to face it, Ethan, for my own sake. And then I have to accept it so I can help the kids get through the shock of it."

He knew she was right. As much as he wanted to protect her— and the children—this was the necessary first step in beginning to rebuild. He reminded himself that this family, unlike many of their neighbors, really only faced rebuilding their way of life, and their sense of security in a world gone mad. They'd lost so little compared to the hundreds he'd seen those first awful days of search and rescue. He thought he'd probably take advantage of some of the post-traumatic healing programs they were talking about setting up. He was finding it harder and harder to sleep, or to get those horrific images out of his head, even in the daytime.

"OK, but you have to hang onto me and we're going to take it very slowly. You've made such good progress the last few days, and we all need you back."

She nodded assent, but he could tell from her eyes she heard and saw nothing but the demons she was determined to face, here and now. Soon, they'd come back armed with trash bags and storage containers, still hoping to find those last few things worth saving, but for now they would simply explore and assess. They picked their way carefully through the detritus of once well-ordered lives, here and there augmented by fragments of other lives as well, and stepped into a surreal world. Crossing the front yard, now stripped of bushes and trees and flowers so meticulously cultivated over the years, they slowly, cautiously edged around the huge pile of splintered lumber and rock and brick that had been their home, toward the back yard that was once their recreation and sanctuary. Was it really only a little over a week ago that Ethan had sat watching his little ones play there? Would any of that brick wall that had given him such a sense of security still be standing? He briefly pictured those two breath-taking butterflies, perched like sentinels above where Emmy and E.J. had last played.

"Ethan!" Lizzy's choked voice shocked him out of his reverie.

"Liz! What! Are you..." He turned to examine her face, then followed her astonished gaze. He didn't know whether to laugh or cry. Not only was part of that treasured brick wall still standing, but just past the play yard, in the midst of all the chaos and destruction, stood four young trees, still green and vibrant. The kids' trees! The ones they'd so joyfully planted to celebrate each birth, and so reverently inscribed with a prayer on each birthday! Neither of them had admitted, even to themselves, that the most painful loss of all was those trees; but not a leaf seemed to be missing. How could they have survived untouched when everything around them was destroyed!

In spite of her still-weak legs, Elizabeth was in that little grove of trees in mere seconds, tears of joy streaming down her cheeks. Ethan was right behind her, sharing her joy and her whispered, "Thank You so much, Lord! Thank You!" She slowly ran her hand over each verdant tree, tenderly tracing every prayer, and turned radiant eyes to him.

"Ethan, I feel like God has just given us the sweetest gift! It's like He's reminding us He still holds the future, no matter how it looks to us."

She gingerly lowered herself to the soft grass—inexplicably still lush in that little copse—and he settled beside her. They sat hand in hand, wordlessly allowing this gift of healing to wash over them, knowing that this settled it. Whatever their friends in this decimated neighborhood decided, they would rebuild right here. Liz smiled as she remembered what E.J. had said his "butterfly guy" told him: "....someday they'd have a house he'd like even better than the old one." She doubted that. Too many memories had infused the pores of that comfortable brick-and-stone house. But, she reminded herself, the only way to recovery was forward. They'd make new memories in a new house, and they'd work hard to make it, someday, as comforting as the old. She was just grateful the kids' trees—and the memories—would be there waiting for them.

2:00 p.m.
Wednesday, June 1, 2011

Liz sat on what was left of her front porch, resting her shaky legs. Would she ever be able to run, and garden, and do all those things she loved to do again? It seemed like the muscles she'd taken pride in keeping toned had turned against her. She couldn't even stay upright long enough to begin building them back. She ran her hand over the smooth stone beneath her, remembering how carefully she'd selected each of its companions, overseeing their installation with such intensity that Ethan had cautioned, to her embarrassment, that she was "driving the stone-masons nuts!" Well, she thought, they'd been avenged! Only a few of those treasured stones remained. Amazingly, they'd found the massive one she'd chosen for the front entry in a neighbor's yard a block away. Unbroken! How terrifying to think of the power it took to rip that colossus from its concrete bed and carry it so far and then set it down whole. And how gratifying to know it had done absolutely no harm to anyone, or anything, in its improbable flight. She really hoped they could retrieve it and use it for their new place. It seemed somehow comforting to think that it might someday welcome them home again.

She sighed, closing her eyes against the discouragement she was feeling. Everything was just too overwhelming! How could she even begin to pull their lives back together and plan their new home when she couldn't even get her legs to work like they should? She knew her husband was right; their family had so much more on which to rebuild than many in this stricken community. They were all alive and recovering from their injuries, but every day they heard more stories of indescribable losses their people had endured: of husbands who died protecting their wives; of one child ripped from a mother's arms while another remained; of injuries too horrendous to contemplate. The death count today was somewhere around 135 souls, and still rising. Frantic families across the area were still searching for missing loved ones, still hoping… somehow… She thought of E.J., stumbling out of that cloud of debris, and prayed there would be still more miraculous returns.

Familiar voices penetrated her sorrow. What was it the famous old baseball manager said? "It's déjà vu all over again?" There on the curb below, like apparitions from a happier past, sat Elly and Ali, black hair against blonde, deep in conversation. Liz fleetingly longed for those little-girl giggles that were always such a part of their chatter. There would probably be few giggles today, though. She knew both girls had dreaded this first return to their roots, even as they looked forward to it with excitement. Ali had been such a constant presence in their home; Liz knew she was grieving the same losses her friends were. She reminded herself to be especially sensitive to her "other daughter" today. Ali had unquestionably suffered the most egregious injury of all; she was still frequently in pain, and there was still no assurance her arm would ever be normal again. Liz sometimes thought she discerned a degree of brittleness under that determinedly sunny facade, and she knew from her own experience that seeing their home and neighborhood so completely decimated was harder than one could imagine. She hoped she and Ethan had made the right decision to bring them here, and to let them discover for themselves the "miracle of the trees." She was still just amazed that little grove had survived intact. Oh, she and Ethan both knew tornadoes were notoriously capricious, often selecting with precision what to destroy and what to leave untouched. But, in their heart of hearts, they were convinced their compassionate God had guarded those beloved trees as His promise of tomorrow for their family; and even sweeter, His reminder that their first-born son was flourishing in Heaven, as his tree was here on earth.

With nothing to block her view, she could see their SUV as it turned onto their street several blocks away. A wave of nostalgia washed over her. One of the things that had drawn them to this neighborhood had been the beautiful old trees. Now they were gone! Houses could be replaced fairly quickly, but these streets would not be lined with such luxurious shade again in their lifetime.

Well, Ethan was on his way and she'd better stop moping. Maybe they could spearhead a tree-planting party in the neighborhood in a year or two. That should be a good way to begin rebuilding what had been of much more importance to the neighborhood than trees…

Liz tried not to let the wave of discouragement reassert itself as she leaned heavily on her grandmother's old hand-carved cane, struggling to rise from her sunny perch. She was truly grateful this particular treasure had somehow survived. They'd found it without a scratch on it, standing upright in what was left of the children's play yard like some atavistic promise of better days to come. But she was not quite successful in extending that gratitude to her need for it. Somehow, during all her morning runs when she'd carried it as a defense against over-enthusiastic neighborhood dogs, she'd never pictured herself needing it for support and, to her shame, she realized it embarrassed her. "OK, Elizabeth," she muttered through clenched teeth. "If Alison can accept that hot, itchy, heavy cast and that metal frame around her waist with such good humor, you'd better learn to accept a little restriction in your mobility with at least half her maturity!" So, by the time their battered vehicle pulled into the drive, three smiling women greeted its driver with hugs of welcome.

Ethan and Liz sat watching Elly and Alison pick carefully through the rubble. They'd all agreed this was probably where Elly's room had been, and, with the confidence of youth, the girls were certain they'd find something. Ethan prayed they would—it seemed so important to both of them. His heart went out to them; he certainly knew what it was like to long for something that might restore a little continuity to their lives.

He started toward them in alarm as they started digging excitedly. He'd warned them he wasn't sure how stable those ruins were and they certainly did not need another injury in this family! Then he stopped, letting their poignant tableaux play out: excited but careful high fives; the "Elly/Ali traditional victory dance;" an even more careful hug; then giggles. Ethan thought he'd never again complain about little girl giggles—or big girl ones. Right now he thought it was the sweetest sound in the world. Elly turned toward her parents, eyes brighter than he'd seen in days, triumphantly waving a book. Her journal! Probably only her father understood how much she treasured that leather-bound tome, filled with her most intimate, heart-felt thoughts. He'd given her the binder, gold pen engraved with "Elly-bug" in its pen holder, when she was only ten years old. He could still see those huge green eyes as he handed her the matching, well-worn one *his* father had given him when *he* was ten and told her she was old enough now to read some of his entries. As far as he knew, she'd faithfully written something every night until it was lost in the storm. He glanced at his wife and saw her tears of gratitude mirroring his own. There could not have been a more priceless find!

"Dad!" He was by their side in a moment, ready to save them from whatever snake or spider or other menace had taken up residence in their home.

"No way!" There, face down in the rubble was Elly's dresser, and beside it, as if some unseen hand had carefully lined them up, was her bureau. Friends who had previously searched the site had missed them because of the sheet of insulation board that somehow, from somewhere had covered them, creating a perfect shield against rain and damage. They hadn't even gotten wet! "OK, Muscles. He-e-e-ave ho! Let's see what we can salvage here."

He helped Elly carry the drawers, one at a time, to the shady grove where her mother and best friend now sat, thoroughly enjoying the excitement. As they made the second trip, Elly suddenly stopped, mouth open, wide eyes darting from tree to tree, then parent to parent. Every possible emotion raced across her expressive face. A look of utter delight quickly replaced her initial one of shock. A smile began in eyes brimming with tears and enveloped her face, finally reaching her lips, where it seemed it would split her delicate features in two. All other treasures forgotten, she slowly moved toward her family's "miracle trees," reverently caressing each one, stopping to lay her cheek on the one they'd dedicated to Eagan sixteen years ago.

She sometimes wondered if she actually remembered the day that they'd planted his tree with such joy and optimism, or just remembered all the stories they'd shared. She closed her eyes, reveling in its fragrance, feeling it hum with life and hope. Tears that always seemed present in thoughts of her brother slipped unheeded down her cheeks. No one moved in the absolute stillness as she stood, allowing its vibrant freshness to wash away grief and fear and anger she'd kept hidden deep inside. She moved on to her tree then, totally unaware of anything but this place, transported by the promise of life represented here. She relived that morning, twelve lifetimes ago now, when she'd snuggled in her bright room, enjoying the rustle of those leaves outside her window. She slowly traced each prayer her parents had inscribed there, reading them quietly to herself. Then she got to the last one. She'd never seen this one before! A look of wonder filled her eyes and she reached out to her parents, now standing beside her, as she read aloud the one they'd so joyfully inscribed the morning of her graduation: *"May 22, 2011. For I know the plans I have for you, says the Lord; plans for good, and not for evil, to give you hope and a future. Jeremiah 29:11."* She beckoned to Ali, still sitting transfixed on the ground. They'd shared almost every tear and triumph of their young lives. It was only right she be here to share this most important one. The circle of three became four and they stood; arms linked, heads bowed, hearts full of thankfulness too great to be spoken.

It was practical, get-things-done Liz who finally broke the spell. "Well, girls, I guess if any of us ever need a reminder that God truly does 'govern in the affairs of men,' all we need to do is walk out here and spend a few minutes. But I think I heard it's supposed to rain again tonight, so we'd better get whatever we can retrieve today into the car as quickly as we can. Elly, I think your dresser and chest were so protected they probably could be moved to the storage unit and you can just take your time going through things there. Did you see anything else promising in the middle of all that mess?"

The look of excitement in both girls' faces was answer enough.

"My books! It looked like my dresser landed on top of my bookcase, and nothing looked damaged there either. Dad, can you help me see if it can be moved, too?"

As they'd been talking, Ali had wandered back to Elly's tree. She stood a moment studying the limb just above her head, then said softly, "Elly, look! I can't reach it, but…"

Ethan reached to retrieve the gold trinket she had spotted, and this time was rewarded by those cherished giggles from both girls. It was Elly's most treasured piece of jewelry! On their fourteenth birthday, the girls had bought matching lockets proclaiming "BFF" for each other and had seldom been without them since. Elly turned to allow her mother to fasten the gold chain around her neck; then, with a restrained version of their victory dance, the girls celebrated its recovery.

"Frank and Ned are on their way with a trailer, Elly. You're right. It looks like most of your books survived. You can go through your stuff in the storage unit whenever you're ready. I have to give you girls credit. I wouldn't have believed you'd find so much still salvageable. Maybe we'll bring the Little's out tomorrow and hope they'll be so lucky." Studiously avoiding his wife's eyes, he pretended not to hear her stifled protest at the mention of bringing the children out tomorrow. They'd talk about it tonight, but he was convinced it would be best for them to be included in the family's retrieval efforts. "We'd better get back to Carthage. Ginny will have dinner ready before long, and both our 'casualties' need rest. If we send Ali home exhausted tomorrow, we may never get her back down here again."

8

AFTERSHOCK

1:00 a.m.
Saturday, June 4, 2011
McConnell Basement Apartment

"Mom-m-m-e-e-e!" The high-pitched shriek tore through their basement apartment, bringing Liz upright in her bed before she was fully awake. She sat a moment, trying to discern if she'd been dreaming or if one of her children was in distress.

"Mom-m-m-m-e-e-e-e!" There it was again, more frantic this time. She struggled out of bed, careful to make sure her unwieldy legs would support her, and hobbled into the children's room. Elly was already there, rocking her little sister in her arms as she sobbed in terror. Usually Emmy looked to Elly for comfort and refuge as readily as she did her mother, but this was too intense. No one would do but Mommy.

"Mommy's here, EmmaLeah. It's all OK, see? Sissy's here and Bubby's safe in his bed. Did you have a bad dream? Do you want to tell us about it?"

Emma clung tightly to her mother, head buried in her shoulder, and sobbed. "It wuz comin' again, Mommy! Me wuz aw awone in the basemen' and me could hear it, and me cuddn' fine you or Daddy or E.J. or Ewwy or me burfwy guy. Is it comin' again, Mommy? Why di'n't me burfwy guy answer me?"

"It was only a bad dream, Sweetie! C'mon, Elly. We need to take Emmy outside so she can see the beautiful stars and moon tonight. E.J. …?"

E.J. had been sitting quietly in his bed, a slightly bemused look on his face. At his mother's invitation, he scrambled to take Elly's outstretched hand and accompanied them with his usual six-year-old dignity, quickly assuming his self-appointed role as his little sister's protector and advisor. "See Emmy, there's the Big Dipper. Remember when I showed you the other night? Can you find the Little Dipper?"

Emma, usually quick to respond to her brother's attentions, simply clung to her mother and peeked at the sky over her shoulder.

Ethan joined them there on the basement patio, quietly soaking in the fragrance of the night and watching the shadows move as the bright silver moon rose above them. He couldn't help but compare the tranquility of this night to that fearsome one only two weeks ago when "the worst tornado in sixty years" had so abruptly turned their world inside out. He really wasn't surprised that one of the children was suffering some aftershock. To be honest, he was a little more concerned about his stoic, always-dignified son and his responsible-for-everyone daughter than he was his little princess, who unfailingly wore her feelings on her sleeve. He wondered when their time for traumatic reaction would come, and resolved to watch closely for any symptoms he could identify. He was so glad the community was taking steps to provide healing programs for survivors. He thought he just might enroll his whole family. Funny, how experiencing first-hand the vulnerability of the human condition served to break down whatever pride and self-sufficiency one usually hid behind.

"Ali, there's room. Now that you're awake, you might as well enjoy the moonlight, too." Liz had looked up to see her standing at the sliding door, sleepily trying to assess what was happening with her "other family." Ethan picked E.J. up and moved over to the smaller glider so Ali could sit between Elly and Liz. He was gratified to notice how instinctively both women slipped an arm around her, and how her presence seemed to bring Emmy to life. Cautiously the little girl slid over to her lap, taking care not to jostle her cumbersome cast. Since the first time Emma had seen "Sissy's bes' fwiend" with that impressive cast on her arm, she seemed to have appointed herself her personal encourager and sympathizer. Ethan smiled, remembering Elly gently informing her sister that asking Ali how she was feeling was very considerate, but probably once a day was enough.

They sat peacefully, grateful that their family was together, allowing the scents and sounds of the night to heal tired, hurting spirits.

"Dad?" E.J.'s soft voice was almost lost in the darkness.

"Hmmm? What is it, son?"

"Dad, I had a dream, too." It was barely a whisper.

There it was... the first symptom! "Careful, Ethan," he cautioned himself, "don't over-react."

"When was that? Do you want to tell me about it?"

"Yes, but..." He looked meaningfully at the women in the other glider.

"Let's take a walk down to the pond, E.J., just you and me. I want to hear all about it."

They settled on the garden bench by the little fish pond, listening to the music of the rock waterfall. Ethan waited patiently for his son to begin.

"It was really weird tonight when Emmy had the same dream I had last night. At first I thought I was awake and I was all alone and it was dark and it sounded just like the tornado was coming. It was getting louder and louder and I called and called but no one was there. I was so scared. Then I woke up. I tried to remember what my butterfly guy said, that he'd be there whether I could see him or not, but everything was so dark, and for a little while I couldn't even remember where I was. Then I heard you and Mom talking and I felt better..."

"You know you could have called us, E.J."

"I-i-i-i kno-o-o-w, but..."

"Tell you what, son. Why don't we see if Mom can get a night light tomorrow. I'm sure Emmy would sleep better with a little light in the room, and you'd be able to see to help her if you need to. On one condition, though. You have to promise to call us if you have any more bad dreams, and I promise we'll tell you if Mom and I do. What do you think?"

The relief on his son's face touched Ethan's heart. It was becoming obvious the kids had been a little more affected by all they'd been through than it first appeared. Reassured that it was OK to admit he was afraid, E.J. relaxed against his father's shoulder and soon was sound asleep. Ethan sat a little longer in the soft darkness, enjoying the gentle sounds around them, lulled by the peaceful rhythm of his son's breathing.

7:00 p.m.
Sunday, June 5, 2011

Elly paced the floor of her little basement bedroom. It was definitely time she got her head on straight. She and her best friend had survived an EF5 tornado together. They'd celebrated together—and then cried and prayed together for friends who hadn't. They'd shared the excitement of finding Elly's journal and locket and books when Dad had been so sure nothing was left. (He'd tried to hide it, but they'd both known exactly what he was thinking.) And Ali had been there when she'd discovered that "Elly's and Eagan's trees" had survived, too. It was all so amazing! Almost like God had somehow protected the little things that really mattered to each of them. She shuddered. Things could have been so different. Why couldn't she just be grateful for this week?

She'd been almost relieved last night when the Wilson's had called to say they were coming to get Ali. Elly had seen her getting more exhausted each day, and there was no question the time had come for her to be home where she could rest and heal. Lunch today had been such a therapeutic time for all of them. So good for both families to relax and laugh and joke together again. She thought maybe she loved Ali's family almost as much as she loved her own.

Of course she already missed her friend, but they both needed space now for the battles they were facing. There would be time for several more visits before they started college in the fall, so why that sinking feeling in the pit of her stomach when they left this evening?

She slid to the floor and sat propped against the door, arms around her knees in an instinctive gesture of self-protection, staring at the exceptionally garish painting Ali had insisted was a "must-have" for her new room. They'd found it a few days ago at an estate sale, marveling that there still actually were such normal, everyday activities in this grief-scarred land. A smile touched her lips. They'd laughed till they'd cried, reliving the solicitous sales manager's not-so-subtle concern that this poor, disabled young woman was making a very un-artistic choice. And they'd dissolved into hysterics picturing how that kind man would have reacted if he'd learned this poor, disabled, very un-artistic young woman would one day be teaching impressionable young minds that very subject! They'd studiously avoided looking at each other as he'd tried to gently steer her toward the painting beside it. There were actually a lot of nice pieces in the estate, he'd confided earnestly. Had she noticed this beautiful landscape? It was an original, signed by one of the area's best-known artists. Elly had just stepped back and watched as this "poor disabled young woman" charmed the man into not only selling her that atrocious painting for $5.00, but throwing in the "beautiful landscape" for good measure, and then an hour or so later, graciously loading both in the back of the battered SUV that picked them up.

They'd actually had fun that afternoon for the first time since the tornado, giggling and arguing about just the right spot to hang it, "where Elly would be reminded that things could always be worse!" They'd let their imaginations run wild, trying to picture Aunt Maud, proudly signing that painfully amateurish painting "with love;" envisioning her long-suffering family's search for just the right spot to honor her without totally humiliating them all.

She could still see Ali, dramatically sighting along an up-turned thumb, directing her to "this wall… no, that one," then unconsciously cradling that cumbersome cast as Elly held the painting up for final judgment. Uncomfortably reminiscent, Elly thought, of the moment she'd first seen Ali cradling her shattered arm in an East 20th Street ditch.

That was it, wasn't it! That sinking feeling was fear; but not for herself. Elly was so afraid the pain in which Ali now lived signaled more than just the trauma of bones knitting back together.

"Please, God, no!" her heart begged silently. "She's been through so much. Please don't let her suffer any more."

9

THERE'S JUST SOMETHING DIFFERENT...

Monday, June 6, 2011
Joplin, MO

In the midst of all the heartache, it truly was amazing. In this "Buckle of the Bible Belt," where churches of all denominations were everywhere, churches were becoming *The* Church, united in care for the whole community, truly God's heart and hands to a troubled land.

Though the media that swarmed the area the first two weeks were pretty much off to the next big story, the flood of volunteers seemed to be growing, from every direction. They came from all over the Four-State region, and from places like Vancouver, Canada; and Trenton, New Jersey; and Tuscaloosa, Alabama, still reeling from their own devastating tornado. They came with pickup trucks and sleeping bags and semi-trailers full of donations. All ages came, eager to do whatever was needed. They came to unload trucks and fold donated clothing and help survivors shop for food and supplies in huge tents filling church parking lots, already sweltering in the unseasonable heat. They came each day with breakfast and lunch and snacks for the volunteers; with chain saws and shovels and construction tools and work gloves, to work in areas still piled high with debris and refuse.

Curfews and deadlines for debris removal were set and then revised as local officials struggled to keep up with evolving needs. The stench became unbearable as rotting food, rain-soaked bedding and unrecovered bodies lay trapped in the rubble. Breathing masks were handed out with tools and equipment as reports surfaced of an unidentified, so-far untreatable fungus.

The medical community became organic, old rivalries forgotten in the face of such great need. Joplin's historic Memorial Hall and the two colleges, both of which were mercifully located outside the tornado's path, opened their auditoriums for triage units and clinic areas and information centers. A temporary morgue was set up at the University.

FEMA and American Red Cross trailers shared church parking lots with Convoy of Hope and Samaritan's Purse. Church members were trained as survivor advocates, helping overwhelmed families work through red tape and documentation requirements. Habitat for Humanity announced plans for multiple building projects. And rumors were heard that Extreme Home Makeover would be coming to Joplin.

Ethan knew they would have to spend time addressing their family's needs soon. There were insurance claims and Red Cross forms and FEMA registration to file. Their pile of rubble would have to be sorted and cleared and prepared for pickup. But so much was needed by so many, and it was cathartic to know he was being useful as a volunteer. Elly had also found her volunteer niche, and the drive from Carthage each morning had become a pleasant interlude for both of them. Today it had gone from pleasant to joyful as Liz had joined them for the drive down and taken her place at a volunteer table, helping sort donations. Her delight at the prospect of being able to offer help touched his heart. It was more than just a cliché, thought Ethan, that it was much more blessed to give.

10

MARY-ANN MARIA EMMALEAH
and the SECRETS BOX

11:30 a.m.
Tuesday, June 7, 2011
McConnell property

"OK, kids, let's go over the rules one more time."

"Da-a-ad…"

"Sorry, Son, but this is one time you have to do exactly what we say. That big pile of debris could be dangerous if you aren't careful."

The family sat in the car on their decimated drive, "McDoggles" meals in hand. Elly had suggested they take the children to their backyard grove for a picnic, and Liz had quickly sensed it wasn't only the little ones who might be helped by spending some family time there, so they'd made a quick stop at the surviving Wal-Mart for a plastic tablecloth and paper plates. She still wasn't entirely comfortable with the idea of exposing her babies to the complete destruction of their home; however, she couldn't argue Elly's logic that if they didn't see it, it might be more difficult for them to understand why everything was going to be so different.

"OK, kids. Let's go eat and then you can do some exploring. E.J., you help Mommy around the house to the back and Emmy's going to ride right here on my shoulders. Elly, can you grab the lunch stuff?"

E.J. was so focused on being sure his mom got around the house safely that he seemed not to pay much attention to his surroundings until they rounded the corner. Then the back yard came into view and he stopped, transfixed by the sight of his play yard, now in shambles. Liz watched him closely as, completely uncharacteristic of their "Mr. Responsible," he forgot his assignment as her escort and slowly walked through the chaos, silently surveying his jungle gym and beloved tree house. The huge old tree in which he and his dad had spent last summer building his tree house had been uprooted and lay across the big wooden play gym that had been his fifth birthday present. Liz fought tears as she watched her little boy walk almost reverently to the tree to inspect what was left of his fort. Actually, it was mostly intact. Though the tree had pretty much splintered the play yard, the way it had fallen had protected the wooden structure in its branches. E.J. cautiously climbed into his little retreat, now lying on its side, and emerged with a relieved, victorious look. He caught his father's eye and lifted a small box above his head, like an athlete brandishing his trophy. His "secrets box!"

The little wooden chest, complete with its small antique padlock, had originally been a gift to six-year-old Ethan from *his* father, "to keep all his secrets safe." Ethan had presented it to his own son the day they'd finished his fort. He'd been surprised he couldn't read E.J.'s reaction. Those big brown eyes that were usually so expressive had seemed inscrutable as he'd listened to his father's stories of the secrets box. They'd seemed to widen slightly when Ethan told him he'd left some of his own secrets in the box, but then he'd simply clasped it against himself and wordlessly disappeared into his hideout. They'd only talked about it one other time, when Ethan had suggested he could keep an old coin they'd found in it. He'd been rewarded with that same inscrutable look, and concluded that, in E.J.'s mind, a "secrets box" meant just that: Whatever he chose to keep in that box was *his* secret. Now Ethan was humbled to realize just how important that little heritage box was to his son. E.J. threaded his way carefully back toward his parents, holding the box in that same curious way, almost as if it was clasped to his heart. He stopped before his parents, took a deep breath, and resolutely held the box out to his father. "I was trying to keep it safe so I could give it to *my* son, Dad."

Time seemed to stand still in that formerly well-kept yard as three adults struggled to contain tears that threatened to overflow. Kneeling before his son, Ethan gently placed his hands on his shoulders and said in a choked voice, "I—I can't think of a better thing to do with it, son. That would make me very proud. But I think it would mean more to him if you kept it until you can give it to him. Tell you what, when we get through here we'll find you your very own spot in the storage unit. You can keep it there until we get a new house. Why don't I put it in the car while you help the girls get lunch ready? Then we'll help Emmy see if she can find some of her stuff. "

E.J.'s look of relief told him he'd stumbled into the right response. Sometimes he wondered how he'd ever raise this child who was layers deeper than any child he'd ever known. Thank God he'd had the good sense to marry a woman who was even deeper.

Ethan came back around the house to find his family in their shady grove, seated on the grass around the outspread tablecloth, McDonald's meals ready. E.J. surprised them by volunteering to give thanks, then brought them to tears again by earnestly thanking God for taking care of them so well and giving them everything they needed, "...even stuff we don't really need." The family ate in silence, each lost in their own memories of the past two weeks.

"Mommy?" Emma's wistful little voice brought them back to the present. Liz pulled her onto her lap and rubbed her chin on her daughter's curly hair.

"What, Munchkin? Finished eating already?"

"Mommy, you fink Mewy-Ann Mewia Emmaweah in dere somewhere? You fink she hurt?"

Liz was speechless. In the two weeks since the storm, Emma had never mentioned any of her toys that had always before been absolutely mandatory bedtime companions. "Mary Ann Maria EmmaLeah" was her very favorite, with the red curls and blue eyes of her owner. Though Emmy was satisfied to refer to her other, innumerable stuffed animals and dolls by their generic names, like "bear" or "kitty" or "baby," the little red-haired doll was "named after Emma." No one had ever been able to figure out where the Mary Ann Maria part had come from. Questions about why she always called her by all those names brought only a smile. Finally, at her brother's insistent questioning, Emma had explained defiantly, "'Cause me wike it." Ethan's eyes met his wife's over their daughter's head. "Well, Princess, let's go see if we can figure out where your room was and find out." A caution not to get her hopes up died in his throat. They'd cross that bridge when they came to it.

Emma smiled her sunshine smile and hopped off her mother's lap. "Wight dere! See? Me curtain wight dere!"

She was right! At least that was where her curtain was now. Hopefully it hadn't just been blown there from its normal place by the twister.

"OK, little one. You stay here and take care of Mommy while Elly and E.J. and I see what we can find."

Twenty minutes later a stack of wood and debris lay just beyond what had undoubtedly been a sunny little "Princess" room only a couple weeks before. Ethan and Liz silently prayed at least one of Emma's toys had survived, protected from the coating of insulation and ground glass that doomed so many things that would have been salvageable otherwise. Suddenly E.J. shouted excitedly, "Dad, look! There's Emmy's toy box." From under the rain-soaked mattress, still inexplicably covered by Emma's pink-and-white Cinderella bedspread, a corner of her toy box peeked out. "Please, God, grant that this one time she actually put all her toys in the chest like her mother told her," Ethan prayed silently as he carefully turned the mattress over; assuring the bedspread was turned away from the white-and-gold-painted box beneath. He carried the chest to where Emma waited breathlessly, bouncing up and down on her toes like a ballerina warming up for a performance. Taking a deep breath, he slowly opened the lid, almost afraid to see what it might contain.

"Mewy-Ann Mewia Emmaweah! Mommy, see? Me baby!" Emma's excited cry was like music to the entire family. There, lying sedately on top of the chest crammed with stuffed animals and dolls of all sizes was her little red-haired doll.

"Wait, Sweetie! Let Mommy make sure there's no glass or bad stuff on your toys. If there is, it could make you very sick."

Elly watched her little sister struggle to "be a good girl" as her mother carefully inspected her toys, then light up like a tiny sunbeam when her mother smilingly handed over her beloved Mary Ann Maria Emmaleah. She cuddled the doll to her, lovingly crooning, "Oh, Mewy

Ann Mewia Emmaweah. Me miss you so much! Wuz you 'cared? Me too, but we OK now. Me take care uh you, and Mommy an' Daddy take care uh bof uv us!" Then, with her sunniest smile, "An' me burfwy guy take care uh all uv us!"

Two more hours of cautious searching had uncovered more toys and a few useable items from both children's rooms, almost all the treasures from E.J.'s tree house, several more items of Elly's and Liz's jewelry and cosmetics, and, at the very bottom of Emma's toy box, Ethan's journal! Of course! The night before the twister hit, he'd read her a story he'd written in it as a child and then laid it on her dresser. She must have put it in her toy box Sunday morning when Liz sent her to put her toys away.

He had to admit, he was as glad to find it as his kids were their treasures.

Now, exhausted but happy, the family headed for the storage unit, feeling richer than they ever had before.

11

A LIFE WELL LIVED

7:20 a.m.
Wednesday, June 8, 2011
McConnell Basement Apartment

"Elly. We have to leave in about ten minutes. Ready?"

That was strange. She was usually up and ready to go before anyone else. "Elly? You OK?" Liz could have sworn she heard a muffled sob. Well, Elly had been so amazingly strong; it wouldn't be surprising if she crashed at some point. "Elly?" She wasn't even paying attention to Liz's knock. "Elly!"

She tried never to violate her children's privacy, but she couldn't just stand out here when one of them was in distress, and it was obvious Elly must be. She slowly pushed the door open; almost afraid of what she might see. Elly sat, still in her pajamas, cross-legged in the middle of her bed, tears streaming down her cheeks.

"Elly! What in the world is wrong! Has something happened?" No response. The vacant look on her daughter's face was almost frightening.

Liz crossed to the bed and gently shook her shoulder, heart in her throat. Had Elly had a complete breakdown? She'd never seen her like this. "Elly! You're frightening me! What's wrong?" Finally, Elly slowly turned to look at her mother with dead eyes.

"Ali..."

"What? What's happened to Ali?" Now Liz's alarm shifted to the young woman who'd been such a constant part of their family. Surely, with all that child had been through... "Sweetie, tell me, what..."

Then the dam broke. Sobs wracked Elly as she blindly reached for her mother. Liz simply sat on the bed, holding her until the storm had passed. Then the anger came. Green eyes darkened and flashed with fury as she shouted, "It's just not fair, Mom! She's already been through so much, and now this! How could God let it happen? It's just so wrong!"

Her father slipped quietly to the other side of her, and the tears began again as she dove into his arms. His questioning look over her head was answered with a similar one from his wife. And so they sat for what seemed like hours, waiting. Instinctively they knew these tears, as painful as they were, would provide the open door they needed to help her through whatever crisis had just occurred.

Finally, she extricated herself from her parents' embrace and walked to her door, checking to see if her little brother and sister's door was closed. "Just like Elly," her mother thought. "Making sure her family is protected, even in the midst of obvious heartache." She closed her door and leaned against it, as if she had no strength to move further. Liz restrained her mother's instinct to run to her, to *do* something about her daughter's pain, but this was obviously much bigger than she could fix.

"G-Paw Ed..." She faltered and caught the sob before it could escape. Ali's family had called her grandfather "G-Paw Ed" since before she was born, and Elly had begun calling him that the first night she spent at her best friend's house. She'd been a first-grader on her first big adventure away from home, and somehow G-paw Ed had known exactly what to say to help her through those first scary hours. She still remembered how he'd laughed with delight and hugged her when she'd asked timidly, "Can I call you G-Paw Ed, too?"

"G-Paw Ed... was... killed by a drunk driver last night." She stood, eyes closed against the desolation in her heart. "He was coming home from Ali's Aunt Victoria's and a pickup crossed the center line and hit him head on. They said he never even knew what hit him, but..." She shuddered and slowly opened eyes swimming in grief. "Mom, she never cried for herself. Through all the surgeries and physical therapy—and I know she's still in a lot of pain—Ali never once said 'Why me?' or complained about how miserable she was. But when she called this morning… I've never heard anyone cry like that. I just thought I couldn't stand it. I have to go be with them."

"Of course you do," her father agreed. "You can take the SUV. Stay as long as you need to. I can borrow Frank's pick-up until you get back."

She slid down to sit against the door then, arms encircling her knees in that self-protective ritual, downturned eyes shaded with something Ethan couldn't quite read.

"I can't." She looked up in anguish. "Dad, I have to make myself get in the car every morning. I just keep reliving that night, and if I even think of trying to drive again, my heart feels like it's going to pound out of my chest."

Liz did go to her then, uncooperative legs forgotten as she slid down beside her and wordlessly took her hand.

"Baby, I'm so sorry. You never… I had no clue." Her father's voice was thick with regret. "Well, we'll work on that as soon as you get back, but I think right now we'd better see if the Zimmerman's can entertain the Little's again while your mom and I take you to the Wilson's. We need to see what we can do to help, anyway. Maybe you should take a few things in case you decide to stay awhile."

"Thanks, Dad. I know it will help Ali for you to be there. You know she feels like you and Mom are part of her family. I'll call and tell her we're on our way. I can be ready in about thirty minutes."

9:30 p.m.
Highway 69

It had been such a hard day! Liz and Ethan were both exhausted as they drove back to Joplin late that evening. They'd return for the funeral in a few days and bring Elly home, but they'd felt it was time for them to give the heartbroken family space to deal with all that this tragedy had imposed on them. Ali seemed inconsolable. The loss of her grandfather had shattered that brittle façade of determined cheer, and the tears just would not stop. She clung to Elly like one clings to a lifeline and in the face of such need, Elly seemed to grow in strength and courage before their eyes. She would be all that her friend needed in the days ahead. But Ethan was troubled. Her confession this morning about driving worried him. To him, it seemed to portend deeper problems, and he wondered what price this time of shouldering her friend's heartache would exact on her already fragile spirit.

9:00 p.m.
Saturday, June 11, 2011
Highway 69

The funeral had been a true celebration of life well lived. The family had been shocked to find that Ed Wilson had, at some time in the past few years, made all the arrangements for his own "going home celebration."

"No tears for me, please!" he'd written in his "to-be-read-upon-my-death" letter to them. "By the time you read this I'll be dancing down those golden streets with my sweet Sarah and talking to my Jesus face to face. Just be sure you plan to meet me there someday." And this mandate was also in writing: Absolutely NO eulogy, thank you—people either knew who he was or it didn't matter. Songs of joyful praise ONLY, please—he planned to be celebrating. And, instead of wasting time talking about him, please read his personal letter to each member of the family. Each one brought tears and laughter, and Ethan's heart was touched when, to their surprise, the minister read G-Paw Ed's letter to "his other grandkid, Elizabeth McConnell."

Since his wife's lingering death from Alzheimer's five years ago, Ed Wilson had thrown himself into working with disadvantaged youth and needy families, many of whom his family didn't even know until they showed up at his memorial this morning. To his family's credit, each one was welcomed graciously and invited to stay for the family meal after the service, which, like so many such gatherings, had been a bittersweet time of laughter and tears as the family drew together and reminisced about G-Paw's foibles and idiosyncrasies and celebrated his strength and legacy.

Ethan stole a glance in the rearview mirror at his daughter, curled up in the back seat, sound asleep. Both parents had been shocked at the dark circles under her eyes when they'd arrived that morning, and

Ethan resolved to get her to a counselor as soon as he could. There was a storm brewing in that wounded heart and he wanted to be ready when it came.

Ali, on the other hand, seemed to have drawn strength from her friend's loyalty and appeared more whole and free than she'd been since the tornado, almost as if her unbridled grief for her grandfather had released her from her self-imposed stiff upper lip.

12

BUTTERFLIES in the MOONLIGHT

Midnight
Sunday, June 12, 2011
McConnell Apartment

Liz and Ethan came awake at the same time. The voice was Elly's, but it seemed to be coming from a distance. And there was an intensity in it that was disturbing. Both parents slipped from their bed to the sliding door of their basement patio. It stood slightly open, so they moved silently to the chairs at the iron-and-glass patio table. The voice seemed to rise and fall, as if its owner was moving rhythmically toward them and then away. They could hear occasional snatches of conversation with... whom? Liz identified it first. A Psalm. Elly was reciting a Psalm. They couldn't hear the words well enough to tell which one, but the intensity and passion in her voice were unmistakable. Now they saw her in the moonlight, pacing around the fish pond in the little valley at the back of the yard. Suddenly, she stopped, fist raised to the sky, and the voice rose until they could hear every word distinctly.

"Why, God? Where are You? Why can't I find You? The world is just upside down and I don't know where to turn because I don't know where You are. Are You hearing me? What do I do with this guilt? She doesn't deserve to be hurting just because she's my friend! It should have been me—not Ali! Why didn't You protect her? You could have stopped us before we drove into that storm! Why didn't You send Big Michael sooner? I know he could have kept her from getting hurt! She didn't want to leave the store. I just had to be Miss Braveheart and show how responsible I was. *I'm* the one. So if one of us had to be hurt, why her? And now why have You taken G-Paw Ed!? She needs him. We need him. We need YOU! I NEED YOU! WHERE ARE YOU! WHY CAN'T I FIND YOU WHEN I NEED YOU SO MUCH? I

WANT TO BELIEVE YOU LOVE ME, BUT WHY? Why-y-y...?"
She crumpled to the ground then, sobbing "Why?" over and over.

Ethan stopped Liz with a hand on her arm as she started to rise.
"Not yet. This is between Elly and God, and He'll take care of her. This
may be the healthiest thing we've seen. I know it's hard, but we need to
let Him play this out." As he saw the look in his wife's eyes he added,
"Of course, nothing says we can't sit here in the moonlight for a
while..."

Elly lay on the bank of the little pond so long they would have
thought she was asleep if it were not for the muffled sobs. At last, she
struggled to her feet and knelt in the moonlight, praying to the God she
finally knew was there.

They could tell as she walked slowly back to the patio this was a
different Elly from the one who'd wrestled there on the pond's bank.
She didn't really seem surprised to see them sitting there; just
wordlessly pulled a chair between them and quietly took their hands.
And there they waited, letting the cool night air wash over hearts that
finally, hopefully, were beginning to heal.

"Mom, I know now God was hearing me, even when I was
shouting at Him and couldn't find Him. I do know He's been so good to
us. Even G-Paw Ed's death turned out to be a blessing for someone. Did
you know Ali's dad plans to ask the court for clemency for the kid who
was driving that truck? He's barely seventeen and he has no family at
all and they heard he's almost suicidal, so Mr. Wilson went to see him.
He said he couldn't sit still and let such a young man's life be ruined
just because he'd been stupid—that G-Paw Ed wouldn't want that. Can
you imagine? No wonder Ali's such an awesome person!

"But I still can't stop thinking about all the people here with
such awful stories that *don't* have happy endings. God says He doesn't
play favorites, so why did He protect us and not them? I just feel so
guilty. Why did He send 'butterfly guys' to protect our kids and let a
single mom lose two of hers? How could He let a new mother and baby
die and leave a new father all alone, especially when they'd dedicated
their lives to His work? Why would He let little children be so horribly
injured? How do you trust a God who chooses to save one person's

grandchild—and her bunny—but not another's son? I just can't make sense of it all and I still get mad at Him if I let myself think about it."

Her mother traced a gentle caress along her arm—an "I love you" that had calmed her daughter's spirit since she was a baby. "I don't think we'll ever find answers that will satisfy our human hearts, Sweetie. Who could ever make sense of the senseless? There are just some things we can't possibly understand, and for some reason, God doesn't seem to think He needs to explain Himself to us." She smiled. "Maybe that's why they call it 'faith.'" She stopped then, lost in her own struggle to accept the unacceptable. "We're already seeing so much good come out of this horrible time, but I know there are 'whys' some people may never work through. I've never been able to find one good thing from losing Eagan, unless it's that Dad and I had to learn to be closer to each other and to trust God more. And, of course, it helps to know He's using us to help others who've lost a child. But would I change it if I could? You betcha! I can tell you this, though. No matter how things look to me, or how mad I may get at Him (yep, I've been pretty mad at Him a few times, especially when Eagan died), I've learned I can trust Him a hundred percent to do what's best for us, whether we understand it or not. I wouldn't want to even get out of bed in the morning if I didn't believe that with all my heart."

Her father's voice was pensive in the quiet night. "I remember reading somewhere that when we get to Heaven all the questions that bother us now won't even matter—or maybe everything will just be instantly clear. I don't know. But I do know this… God is here, and Jesus prays for us! When we hurt, He hurts, and He loves it when we bring our questions to Him. He knows them anyway, but for some reason He wants to hear us speak them to Him, even if we're shouting or sobbing them. I love the Psalm that says He saves all our tears in a bottle. I really think that someday He'll give them back to us as a beautiful gift we can lay at His feet…"

His voice faded into the velvet darkness that wrapped itself around them like a blanket. They lingered there, deep in thought, until suddenly Elly's giggle shattered the silence. "Boy, Dad, you're getting downright poetic in your old age!"

Maybe it was the relief of finally hearing that giggle again, or the joy of their God's presence, or maybe it was just the weariness of frayed hearts, but the giggles were definitely contagious. Soon, all three were laughing so hard Frank and Ginny awakened, wondering if they had three hysterical guests on their hands. And no sooner had they settled around the table with their friends than two sleepy little heads appeared at the door, eager to join this exciting midnight party.

Liz decided she was glad they hadn't slept away this time. There'd be some drowsy people in church later, but the night was just too beautiful to miss, and this little patio was becoming their refuge within a refuge. The scent of just-mown grass and night-blooming flowers surrounded them. Above the little pond, stars twinkling in the midnight sky seemed close enough to touch. Elegant moonflowers gracing the trellised entrance to the patio flaunted creamy trumpets, glowing in the light of the rising moon. She inhaled deeply, drinking in their lemony fragrance.

Ouch! Elly was clutching her arm in an iron grip. Liz darted an alarmed glance at her daughter, now sitting transfixed, staring at the vines loaded with white flowers. There, serenely nestling among those lemon-scented blossoms were two—no, three!—huge Luna moths, translucent wings glistening in the moonlight! She felt a sudden surge of panic. No! Three…? Surely…

Emmy had been dozing in "Unca Fwank's" arms—after the requisite kiss "right there," of course—since she and E.J. had sleepily joined the party. Now she leaned against his chest, watching their ethereal visitors through heavy-lidded eyes. "Such pwetty burfwies! Me wuv burfwies." Her sleepy voice was swallowed by a huge yawn. "Hope me see me burfwy guy again someday."

Liz didn't know whether to laugh or cry. A quick glance at Elly confirmed the same reaction. They stared at each other, embarrassed that they'd so quickly imagined the worst. Butterflies again! Would they ever see one now without that little flutter of fear in the pit of their stomachs?

13

CONQUERING DEMONS

7:30 a.m.
Monday, June 13, 2011
South Range Line Road

Elly took a deep breath. She reminded herself it probably would be hard whenever she decided to face it. But no matter how she tried, she couldn't slow her racing heart. Dad didn't say a word—just laid his open hand between them on the car's seat. She gratefully grabbed that hand that always seemed to be there when she needed it and hung on tight.

Ethan had been deliberately avoiding the worst of the storm area when Elly was in the car; easy enough from Carthage to the church in northeast Joplin. He'd even managed to make the drive to their old neighborhood by going around, not through. But he thought she was strong enough now to confront the memories that awaited her on 20th Street. Apparently, she thought so, too. She was the one who suggested they leave early enough to drive down South Range Line.

He was relieved that Liz had already decided to stay home with the Little's today. It was still a struggle to make her damaged legs support her, and he'd watched her getting more and more exhausted last week. Her mother's heart would break if Elly's battle on 20th Street was as intense as it had been beside the little pond Saturday night, and their daughter needed the freedom to take this next step her way, without feeling she should protect her family.

Mom was right, Elly thought! It was excruciating! No one could describe what she was seeing. The last week or so she'd made herself watch all the coverage on TV, but even that could not begin to convey the sense of helplessness one felt in the face of such crushing loss. The devastation was unimaginable! There was nothing left of familiar landmarks—not even any street signs to direct them. They had to be getting close to 20th Street, but where was the strip mall where she'd almost stopped for refuge? The air left her lungs as the SUV slowed and turned right off Range Line. Dear God! The strip mall had been right here, but it was gone! Nothing was left but piles of rubble. What would have happened to them if they'd been parked there? Or worse, tried to find shelter inside!

As nearly as she could remember, the drainage ditch wasn't very far off Range Line. It must be just ahead. But at the last minute, she couldn't do it! Just couldn't make herself look at that concrete culvert where her best friend's life had hung in the balance. She kept her eyes straight ahead, numbed by the controlled confusion around her. Traffic moved at a crawl as National Guard, police, firefighters, even private citizens with vests that said "TRAFFIC" struggled to keep them moving safely through tortured streets littered with what was left of everything her city had built over several lifetimes.

Bless Dad's heart! He didn't say a word, just kept slowly driving west. Past the shattered church building on Indiana and the crumbling shell of Joplin High. She didn't dare look at the vaunted "HopE High" sign; it would be her undoing. They passed the wreckage of Dillon's Supermarket, where some had died and others were miraculously spared; through huge piles of rubble that had been a residential area; to an older residential area farther in where some homes stood untouched as their neighbors' were damaged or destroyed.

They turned south on Main Street, and she gasped in surprise. Why was no one talking about this? There was nothing left here, either! Blocks of businesses—many handed down from father to son—lay in desolate ruin. Where were the trucks and machines and volunteers dedicated to restoring what was lost? It was every bit as bad as Range Line, but these blocks seemed almost abandoned.

Now, looking west one could see the spectral shell of St. John's in the distance. Every school and church and apartment building and medical office and tree between was gone. Only the cross of St. Mary's Church still stood, stark against the clear blue sky.

"Dad. Turn around! Go back."

He quickly pulled to the curb, not sure what her tone of voice meant, and looked a question at her.

"Look at that cross! Nothing is left around it, but even after an EF5 tornado, it's still standing. I remember hearing that not one cross fell, no matter how bad the buildings around were hit, but seeing this for myself is pretty breathtaking! I sure don't pretend to understand much of anything in all this madness, but as far as I'm concerned, that's God's statement that He's in control. I think His message is pretty clear and Mom is right: He's always there for us, whether we see Him or not; and we can trust Him one hundred percent, whether we understand it or not. We have to go back to the ditch. I need to face what happened there, and now I think I'm finally ready."

Silently they retraced their journey, this time east on 20th Street until they reached the Range Line intersection. They parked in the strip mall's rubble-covered drive and walked back, Ethan watching his daughter closely as she struggled with emotions he found painful to try to read. She stood at the curb, studying the concrete ditch now filled with debris. Was that metal panel in the rubble the one that had shielded her friend? And that huge log that lay along the shoulder of the ditch… surely she couldn't have moved such a behemoth. She turned slowly and gazed down the street. Was she envisioning the huge man she and Ali still insisted had been their rescuer? His heart broke to think of finding his daughter, standing so alone in the terror and chaos after they had disappeared. Ethan was so thankful he'd been able to find her as quickly as he had, though he still had no clue why he'd decided to try to pick his way down 20th Street.

She turned back to the ditch and shuddered. Ethan knew at that moment she saw once again the gruesome sight of her best friend, calmly straightening her shattered arm, and he quickly slipped his arm around her as she shuddered again, then leaned her head on his shoulder.

"What if her arm isn't OK, Dad? What if she can never use it again? What if they can't save it! How can I live with that?"

"Elly, your mom told me when she was at her lowest in the hospital she clearly heard the warning she gave you about trying to be God applied to herself. I guess I'd just reiterate the same caution. Don't get in His way and try to fix something only He can handle. Ali's doing fine, and she has to let Him help her through whatever the future holds for her. Your job is to trust His goodness and keep on being her friend and encourager. I'm really proud of how well you do that. Now, we probably should go. They'll be wondering about us at the church."

They rode in comfortable silence until Ethan pulled into the volunteer entrance of the parking lot. She stopped him with an outstretched hand as he took the keys from the ignition.

"I want to drive home.

"Surprised, her father hesitated only a moment. Then he kissed her forehead and smilingly handed over the keys to her independence for the second time in her young life.

6:00 p.m.
McConnell Apartment

Liz surprised them with dinner on the patio that evening.

She'd spent the morning by the pond, playing with the children and allowing her tired spirit to be replenished. She sat on the garden bench by the water, watching her babies wade and splash in childish glee, grateful for the energy slowly seeping back into her body, and praying her usual prayer for healing. But this time was different. This time she surprised herself by adding, "Lord, I know there's purpose in everything You do, so..." She hesitated, then plunged on, "...so if You have a purpose for these legs that don't work right, then help me accept Your purpose." What surprised her even more was that she knew she meant it. Funny, but that little prayer had brought her the peace for which she'd been longing since the storm.

The children had played so hard that even E.J. didn't argue when she suggested they all take a nap after lunch, and in moments they were all dead to the world.

She wasn't sure what had brought her awake with a start. The house was quiet. The Zimmerman's were gone for the week and the children were still sound asleep. But something felt strange. Had she heard someone at the door? She moved quickly to the kitchen window that overlooked the garden. And then it hit her. Her legs felt almost normal! Had that slight "pop" she'd felt as she jumped out of bed released something that had been restricting them? She took a few more steps, and could hardly contain her excitement.

"Careful, Elizabeth," she cautioned herself. "Don't get everyone's hopes up if this is just a fluke."

She spent the next half hour gingerly testing her body every way she could think of, and every effort she made just seemed to strengthen her more. Finally, she could stand it no longer. She quietly slipped outside, leaving the sliding door open in case the children wakened. She took a deep breath, and ran! Down the hill to the pond… so far so good, but it was downhill, after all. Around the pond and back up the hill, laughing aloud as legs that just this morning hardly worked at all grew stronger with every step. She looked up to see two round-eyed little faces watching her run. Then they were out the door, running to meet her, matching her laughter with shouts of their own. They danced and played tag and ran races until they dropped, breathless, on the fragrant grass.

Slowly, E.J. sat up, turning earnest brown eyes toward his mother. He reached out and touched her face, as if to reassure himself she was real. "Mom, are you well now? Do you think your legs will keep working OK now?"

The wistfulness in his voice brought a lump to her throat. How much had her precocious little man been worrying about that he'd never shared, even with his father? What price would these children, and all the children in this storm-battered area, continue to pay for forty minutes that had turned their world upside down? Well, she wasn't about to dishonor him by sugar-coating anything.

"I'm not sure, son, but it looks like it. I hope so. Tell you what, let's fix a really nice dinner and surprise Elly and Daddy. But you have to help me keep it a secret until I say. OK?

Of course they would. The McConnell children loved secrets and surprises more than anyone she knew. Except, maybe, their mother...

So, when her older daughter surprised her by proudly driving up the Zimmerman's lane, honking for all she was worth, what could she do but run joyfully out to meet them, E.J. and Emmy scurrying to keep up. Elly forgot her own exciting news as she met her mother on the drive, tears of joy streaming down her cheeks.

"Mom! Look at you! What happened?"

E.J. just couldn't contain himself any longer. "Dad! Mom can run!"

"Yeth, yeth, yeth,' Emma chimed in. "We wunned an' danced an' pwayed tag..." She stopped, remembering their promise. "OK to say now, Mommy?"

Ethan laughed through his own tears as he picked up his little girl and danced up the drive with her, singing, "Mommy can ru-un. Mommy can da-ance. Mommy played ta-ag. But Mommy can't keep a secret!"

Liz couldn't remember a more joyful time of thanksgiving for their family. They celebrated Elly's courage and liberation. They celebrated Mommy's "wegs." They celebrated the wonderful meal. They celebrated the phone calls Elly made to Big Mike and Gran, and the texts she excitedly shared with Ali. And they celebrated the joy of just being family.

Elly insisted she and the kids clean up after dinner so Mom and Dad could take a walk around the pond. No argument. Now, go...!

They sat by the pond as the sun went down. Ethan joyfully described Elly's metamorphosis on 20th Street. Liz told Ethan about the prayer that had surprised and freed her. Did he think it had anything to do with her sudden healing? As they strolled back to the house they agreed there was no way they would ever know for sure, but that was OK. They knew the Healer.

While they'd been at the pond, Elly had not only cleaned the kitchen, but put two very tired Little Mac's to bed. They were already sound asleep, and she was engrossed in bringing her journal up to date, so Liz and Ethan headed for the patio to enjoy the night sounds they found so soothing. Though she longed for her own home again, Liz realized she'd miss this peaceful retreat. It had become their haven in every storm, and she thought she and Ethan owed their friends a debt they could never repay.

2:00 a.m.

"I don't know what happened to it, El!"

"Wh-what? Ali? Are you OK? What time is it?

"Oh, Elly! I'm so sorry! I didn't even look at the clock…"

"'Sokay, Al. Don't worry, I can sleep in tomorrow—uh, today, I guess. So, what's going on? Did you have another nightmare? What happened to what?"

"My car! So much has happened I hadn't even thought about it, but… what do you suppose happened to my car?"

"Omigosh! I can't believe none of us even thought about it! What are your folks saying?"

"Haven't talked to them about it yet. They've been pretty much overwhelmed, worrying about my arm and you all. And then, of course, G-Paw…"

Elly tried to swallow the lump that suddenly constricted her throat at the mention of G-Paw. "I miss him so much, Al. I know I only saw him every month or so, but there was always something so comforting about knowing he was there…" Mortified at the little sob that accompanied her words, she hesitated. "Go ahead, Dummy," she thought, "make it worse for the friend you've already caused so much pain."

"It's OK, El! I really miss him, too. I'm not sure I'll ever stop wishing I could hear one of his corny jokes just one more time. Sometimes when I can't sleep I still hear him whispering one I'd completely forgotten."

Elly could almost see her friend smile as they both remembered some of those jokes that always brought a groan and a hug from G-Paw's "G-daughters." The silence lasted so long Elly began to think her friend had finally gone to sleep. Then,

"The folks had Aaron out for dinner last night."

"Aaron? Oh, you mean..."

"Yep. The kid who was driving the pickup. At first, I wasn't even gonna be here. G-Paw's funeral was so sweet—it really helped me accept what had happened; and I am glad the folks decided to reach out instead of condemning, but I just didn't think I was ready to go quite that far."

Elly waited patiently through a second silence. "I'm so glad I stayed, El. He's a really sweet kid, and he's so lost. I can't imagine what his life has been like—he's been on his own since he was ten! He's just so, so sad and ashamed about what happened. When Dad asked if they could pray for him he cried and cried. Dad's meeting him for lunch every week, and he's trying to get him enrolled in a GED prep class. He's convinced Aaron has real potential if they can just get him through the next few years. I kept thinking about some of the things your dad has said about what your grandparents did for him after his parents were killed. Wouldn't it be awesome if someday Aaron could say the same thing?"

The silence this time was comfortable as both girls contemplated the mystery of tragedy being turned to good in unexpected ways.

"Well, OK... back to my car..."

"I'll talk to Dad today, Ali. He has a good friend on the Joplin Police Department. Ron will probably be able to track it. I wonder if someone just saw it sitting on the Books-a-Million lot and decided no one would miss it. I think if the city had towed it someone would have contacted you; though they still have their hands pretty full and probably one car no one's asking about isn't very high on their list of priorities. Can you fax your registration or insurance papers? That might help. I still can't imagine how all of us could have just forgotten it. Shows how important stuff is in the grand scheme of things, doesn't it."

14

A DECLARATION of ENDURANCE

Monday, July 4, 2011
Landreth Park

They were calling it a "Declaration of Endurance." Elly thought she'd never been prouder of her hometown.

For years, the Fourth of July had seen thousands of area residents converge on Joplin's Landreth Park for an old-fashioned day of celebration. Food and game vendors would begin rolling in their portable stands a day or so before, while city workers barricaded Murphy Boulevard, roped off parking areas and moved in essentials like trash barrels and port-a-potties for the revelers who would come to spend the day lounging on blankets or lawn chairs, shooting firecrackers and bottle rockets, eating hot dogs and snow cones, listening to patriotic music and local bands and the national recording artist of the day, and staying to ooh and ahh as the huge fireworks display lit up the darkening sky.

This year it would have been so easy to simply cancel. Hot dry weather had quickly followed the drenching rains that had made it so hard for workers sifting through the mountains of rubble and debris. FEMA trailers were being moved in as quickly as possible, but many families were still living with friends or relatives, or sheltering in relief centers still dotting the city. Municipal leaders were struggling to establish guidelines for disposal of trash and debris, and ensure the safety of workers in the disaster zones. A "tent city" had sprung up on the banks of Shoal Creek just south of town, and local homeowners were beginning to complain of fights and disturbances and concern for small children living there in the sweltering heat. Volunteers were still streaming into the city, and while everyone was more than grateful for their concern and assistance, their presence brought extra pressure on already scarce housing. And the mysterious fungal infection, still unidentified and incurable, was menacing workers in the disaster zone unlucky enough to sustain an open wound.

It would have been so much easier just to call it off, but this year like never before, Joplin needed a time of community and restoration and encouragement.

So the "Declaration of Endurance" was on; and nationally acclaimed talk show host and Missouri native Rush Limbaugh was coming to town with a semi-trailer full of his just-introduced bottled iced tea; free to all as long as it lasted. Parking was at a premium, spilling into the lower fields of Ozark Christian College and then onto their paved lots on the hills above the park. Music was turned to head-pounding volume. Patriotic hats and T-shirts proclaiming sentiments like: "We Are Joplin," "Restore Joplin," "Hope for Joplin" and "God Bless the USA" filled the hot, dusty fields. Late comers found themselves lucky to find a spot for their chairs at the far end of the park, and 35,000 Missourians of all ages mostly displayed a courtesy and consideration of others that would have made their mothers proud.

The guest of honor thrilled the crowd with his love for America and a fifteen-minute tribute to Joplin's courage and spirit. Then he was gone, swinging his beautiful plane over the park for one last tip of the wing to the cheering crowd. Later it was discovered that his new wife had quietly spent the day at the park, charming and encouraging and graciously granting pictures with all who asked.

Elly was amazed that Alison had decided to come. The heat was always a problem for her heavy cast, and though she seldom mentioned it, Elly knew her arm had never stopped hurting.

E.J. and Emma had been so excited that Elly was taking them along to pick her up in Kansas that they slept very little the night before. Both were asleep almost before they left Joplin, and their sister had to admit she appreciated the peaceful drive to Ft. Scott. The drive back was a different matter. The children were inordinately concerned about Ali's arm and outdid each other trying to make her laugh. Both teenagers found their fraying spirits lifted by Little Mac antics, and by the time they pulled into the crowded parking area, all four were ready for a much-needed day of fun.

The girls lounged in their lawn chairs, watching E.J. and Emmy play happily with the children "camped" next to them. Mom and Dad would be along later, but Elly was glad they'd agreed to let the Little's come early. Their parents really needed some time just for themselves, and the kids were having so much fun.

She was impressed with the teen-age boy who seemed to have appointed himself entertainer for a whole crowd of little ones. As they watched him patiently teach them to throw his Frisbees, Ali suddenly sat straight up in her chair, staring over Elly's head as if she'd seen a ghost.

Elly turned in alarm, looking for the reason for her reaction.

"Elly! It's my car! I'm positive! There's the dent we put in the right front fender on your mailbox. They even still have the little bear G-Paw gave me hanging from the mirror! What should we do?"

"Look away, Al. If they're around, don't spook them. I'm calling Dad right now. He said he talked to his JPD friend about your car. I'll bet he's here on duty, and he'll take care of it."

It seemed like forever to the anxious girls, but it was actually only a matter of minutes before they saw Ron strolling casually toward them. Like every other officer in the area, he was on crowd control, though he wore a "Joplin Proud" tee like so many others in the throng.

He smiled his reassurance. "Just be cool, Ali. I've already alerted several of the guys. They'll be watching for whoever is driving that car. Are you absolutely positive it's yours?"

Ali pointed out the fender they'd dented when they turned into the McConnell's mailbox post a couple weeks before the storm, and the "Ft. Scott Honor Student" sticker her dad had sneaked onto her bumper just before graduation. G-Paw's little bear would be "the nail in their coffin," she thought, because he'd actually had her initials embroidered on it.

"Stay here," Ron ordered as he circled around to approach the car from the opposite side. Elly saw him speaking into his walkie-talkie as he walked, and fervently hoped some of "the guys" were close.

They tried to be discrete, but they couldn't resist watching as he talked to the family sitting near the car. The older man listened, nodded, and walked slowly to the car with Ron. They stood talking quietly, and then the man took out his billfold, obviously showing Ron his identification. Two younger men who'd been approaching the car noticed the exchange and quickly reversed course, right into the path of a couple of Ron's "guys." Later, he told them the younger men were neighbors of the family and had been trying to sell them the car. It would have to be impounded until all the evidence was gathered and logged, but Alison would soon have her car back, minus the window the men had broken getting in.

10:00 a.m.
Friday, July 29, 2011

Elly was excited! Ali had called. Her appointment for a smaller cast was next week, and she thought Elly might want to drive her to KC.

Of course she would! But she thought she'd detected a note in her friend's voice that hinted at more than a triumphal trip to get rid of that cumbersome contraption around her waist. Ali's response to her query had been enigmatic. No big deal; since she wouldn't be driving for a while yet and her poor little car needed exercise, just thought a road trip would be fun. Could she be here Sunday evening?

Well, OK. For now she'd have to be patient and let Ali deal with whatever was on her mind her way. She was just glad she could be there for her. Maybe it would help ease some of the guilt that still woke her up at night.

9:00 a.m.
Monday, August 1, 2011
Highway 69

Dinner at the Wilson's was always lively. Elly loved the nothing-off-limits, free-for-all conversation at their table, and last night had been no exception. They'd laughed about G-Paw Ed's wisdom, so

111

often wrapped in silly jokes. They'd grieved for Aaron's anguish and unfolding need. They'd laughed again at G-Paw's little notes, still showing up in most unlikely places. And Elly had been pretty sure she wasn't the only one who saw the shadow...

She hadn't been entirely surprised when, soon after dinner, Ali had pleaded exhaustion and gone to bed early. Now she watched her friend out of the corner of her eye as she drove. The shadow was definitely there behind those usually-lively brown eyes. Was Ali worried about what they might find when they removed that formidable cast today? Was she thinking maybe the constant pain really was a sign her arm wasn't healing, in spite of what the doctors said? Was she concerned about how she would manage school with all the doctors' appointments and therapy that lay ahead? Whatever it was, for the first time Ali wasn't ready to share, and for the first time, Elly had no idea how to reach her.

11:00 a.m.
Kansas City, MO

"O-okay, Alison. With the damage your arm sustained, it's no surprise you're still feeling quite a bit of pain. I wish your arm was healing a little faster, but the x-rays look good and I don't see any reason we can't go ahead with a cast you can wear in a sling. You'll rest better, and it should free you up to attend classes this fall. Let's get you plastered up and you girls can go to lunch.

2:30 p.m.
Highway 69

Elly glanced at her friend, sleeping fitfully in the other seat. Her heart ached to do something... anything. Ali had been absolutely white when they'd finished her cast, and Elly hadn't been surprised when she confessed it really, really hurt. By the time the girls had gotten to the car, she'd seemed to have only enough energy to mumble a faint apology before she drifted off.

Good! There was the Fulton city limits sign—just ten more miles to the Wilson's. Elly breathed a sigh of relief. She really needed to talk to Ali's mom. Something was definitely wrong...

"No-o-o-o! No no no-o-o-o!"

Elly jumped as Alison shot straight up in the seat, eyes wide and unseeing, body rigid and trembling.

She quickly pulled into Fulton and stopped. "Ali! What's wrong? Ali!"

As Ali's eyes came slowly into focus, she took a deep, shuddering breath and collapsed against the seat.

"Oh, Elly. The nightmares are getting worse! I'm almost afraid to go to sleep."

"Ali! Why didn't you tell me about the nightmares? When you were down the last time you seemed great. I had no idea."

"I know. I thought it would just go away. At first it was only once in a while. But since I came home it's the same dream almost every time I go to sleep."

Elly waited, unconsciously stroking Ali's good arm in the comforting ritual that never failed to calm her own spirit.

Ali stared straight ahead, seeing only the dark visions that haunted her nights. "I'm at Books-a-Million and you and G-Paw are waiting for me in my car. I know you are, but you're laughing at his silly jokes and I want to finish my book, so I just keep reading until..." Elly could feel her arm tense as she took a deep breath and struggled for control. "... until I see the tornado. It's heading straight for you but you just keep laughing and talking. I have to warn you, but you won't answer your phone and I can't get the door to open, so..." Another deep breath and then in an agonized rush: "...I can't do a thing but scream and pound on the door while that horrible cloud just picks you up and carries you away."

Now the girls stared at each other, tears streaming down both faces.

"This time it was worse, El. This time the Little's were in the car, too. They were crying and screaming, but you and G-Paw just kept laughing."

She stopped Elly's strangled "Ali..." with a shake of her head, then finished in a dead voice, "The worst part is, it's my *car* I'm worried about. In my dream I know you are all dead, but I'm just worried about how I'm going to get home now. My head knows it's only a dream, but I'm still so terrified when it's happening, and then I feel so ugly and selfish that all I care about is my car. Elly… I didn't even remember my car was gone for nearly a month. Why do you suppose…"

"Al, we have to promise we'll be more open with each other. And before you ask, yes, I'm having the same problem…though I'm not sure my dreams are quite as creative. They're saying nightmares are just part of recovery after a disaster and there's a survivor workshop next weekend dealing with it. If you feel like it at all, I'm coming up to get you. You can stay over a few days before we have to start getting ready for college. And one thing more; you have to tell your parents. I know your mom is worried. I could see her watching you last night. I just couldn't put it all together."

Elly was rewarded with the first real smile she'd seen in her friend's eyes since she'd arrived. "I'm really sorry you're going through this, too, El, but I have to admit, in a twisted way it helps to know. I'll come for the workshop. I'll try anything that might get me through this—but we have to make a pact: we'll call, day or night, whenever we have a nightmare. 'K?"

1:00 a.m.
Thursday, August 11, 2011
McConnell Apartment

Elly padded quietly through the living room. The patio that fronted their basement apartment was always such a refuge, and right now she needed a refuge. She sighed as she settled onto the glider, oblivious to the night scents and sounds that so often eased her restless heart. How could she sleep when her best friend was still in such pain! Memories were too raw of Ali tossing and turning and moaning through painkillers that still ruled her nights.

Still, she was glad Ali had been here for the workshop. She was so impressed with the quality of programs the city had been offering its hurting citizens. They'd even included sessions for kids, and the Little's couldn't wait until they could go back for more "artist classes." It was gratifying that her friend thought the workshop had helped her "get her head straight." But if her mind and spirit were better, her body certainly wasn't.

They'd all celebrated getting rid of that heavy metal frame, but now it was obvious the smaller, lighter cast had only intensified Ali's misery. As Elly dropped her off at home it was clear her friend was just gritting her teeth and focusing on plans for college; but Elly knew those eyes, and there was rarely much sparkle there these days.

15

IT'S JUST STUFF

2:00 p.m.
Monday, September 5, 2011
McConnell Property

Ethan found her sitting on the wall of their scooped out basement, sobbing as though her heart would break. He wasn't really surprised—he'd seen it coming the past two weeks. He wasn't sure what this new battle was, but he didn't push. He knew his wife would talk when she was ready. He settled beside her, gently slipping an arm around her shoulders, and waited.

"It's just stuff, Ethan! One day it will all be gone anyway, but sometimes it hurts so much to have lost the stuff that connected us to our family history. We've come so far the last few months, and I keep telling myself this is just stupid! But..." A fresh wave of tears overtook her and she melted into his protective embrace, mumbling, "It's just stuff..."

He touched the blue china fragment in her hand. Her great grandmother's china—brought to America with great care, presiding over every family celebration and handed down to each generation—until now. "Where did you find it?"

"I was walking in the back yard and saw it embedded in the ground. We're going to have to police the yard really closely before we let the kids play here again. I think there may still be things buried here we haven't found."

She lapsed into silence again, lost in her thoughts. Finally she said slowly, "It's been really strange the last two weeks. I can't figure out why it's been so hard to see them hauling all that debris away. It doesn't make sense. We can't start rebuilding until it's all gone, but... for some reason I've been feeling like a part of myself went with it."

He didn't respond right away. Finally, he said wryly, "I'm just realizing I've been feeling the same way. It is pretty final, isn't it! Even though it was totally wrecked, it was still our house. As long as it was here there was hope we might find something else important. Now, we really are starting from scratch again. I don't think it's stupid at all, Honey. It *was* just stuff, but it was our stuff, and we didn't agree to have it taken from us. It's probably healthy to admit it and give ourselves permission to mourn the loss."

She smiled then, tracing the scar on his hand. He hadn't even realized he was injured that horrific night until he'd come back to the hospital the next morning and a nurse had noticed it. She shuddered, thinking of that horrible fungus that had attacked open wounds—so grateful he'd been spared. "Wise man, my husband! Wise woman, to have snared such a prize…"

"Well, wise woman, how's this for a little wisdom. We're gonna go pick up the kids—E.J. can miss an afternoon of school—and drive to the lake for a picnic. It's such a gorgeous day, and we need a break. It will all still be here tomorrow."

The last three months had been a blur of paper work, insurance claims, FEMA reports, doctor's check-ups, and decisions. Not long after that momentous day in June when Liz and Elly had so jubilantly overcome their personal demons, Ethan had realized that, now that they were both driving again, it was time to replace the cars that had been destroyed in the storm. They'd been astonished at how hard it was for them to make those decisions. The disaster recovery counselor had explained it was a normal part of the process, but Ethan especially had struggled with it. He'd always been such a decisive personality, and after all, it was only cars! It wasn't hard to decide to keep the faithful old SUV, though. It was worthless as a trade-in, and he found it had become almost a symbol of all they'd overcome. Sometimes, he thought ironically, he was like that car; battered and scarred on the outside, but tougher than he looked and good for a few more miles before the junk pile.

It had been harder than they expected to see Elly pack her shiny new car and head off for college, little brother excitedly riding shotgun, the rest of the family trailing behind in their equally shiny new SUV. It had been especially hard for Elly. They needed her, she'd argued, to help with the Little's until they got the new house finished and all the details of recovery taken care of. It was Big Mike who'd turned the tide. The family had decided to mark the three-month anniversary of the day their world was torn apart by gathering once again at the restaurant just south of the tornado's path. It felt almost like a rite of passage; a time of putting behind them the things they could not change and choosing to look toward the future. He'd waited quietly until the discussion had ground to a stop, then said in his firm, no nonsense style, "Elizabeth, you've done a tremendous job of supporting your family during the worst time imaginable. I truly don't know what they'd have done without you, and I'm very proud of you. But your mother is well now, and you need to step back and be the kid again. The best thing you can do for this family is go to school and have a good time and do all the things an eighteen-year-old girl should do." He leaned forward, drilling her with clear green eyes that looked remarkably like hers. "And don't feel like you have to be God. He's perfectly capable of taking care of your family while you're gone."

No one stirred around the table, not even the little ones, as green eyes locked. Finally, Elly dropped her eyes and said through clenched teeth, "If one more person tells me not to try to be God..." Then, raising eyes sparkling with mischief, she threw herself into the lap of this man she'd idolized since she was a baby and finished brightly, "...I'm gonna think He's trying to tell me something!"

And so it was settled. Elly left the following week

16

ABOUT FRANK

Friday, September 16, 2011
Zimmerman Home

They were all worried sick about Frank. He was obviously losing ground, so thin now it seemed one could almost look right through him. Beneath Ginny's determined good cheer were eyes haunted by past battles and fear of what might come. Myriads of tests had all agreed; no new cancer cells that they could find. But something was definitely wrong. They were leaving for Mayo Clinic today, grateful he'd been accepted, and planning to stay until they found some answers.

The Zimmerman's and McConnell's gathered on the sunny basement patio for brunch. Always good friends, the past four months had drawn them close as family, and they all felt a need to share this time together. Emma had quickly claimed her usual place, settling oh-so-carefully on "Unca Fwank's wap," seeming to sense with the instincts of innocence that things were not as they should be. She sat very still, only moving occasionally to gently pat the bald spot "right there" that earned his little princess her place of honor.

They lingered, reluctant to take this next path that just might lead in ways they didn't like. They talked of Elly's adventures in school, of new friends and unexpected challenges, and the nightmares that still stalked all of them occasionally. They talked of the church, of the huge load their leadership carried for hurting people and new programs planned for tornado survivors. They talked of the house plans Frank's firm had drawn for the McConnell's, and of contractors they were interviewing, and schedules for completion. They talked of Ethan's gratitude that the small business he owned was doing well, even though the staff were all working out of their homes until they could replace the building the tornado had destroyed. They talked of what a blessing this time of house sharing had been for both families. The McConnell's, of gratitude for such a welcoming home away from home and such faithful, loving care for their children during these hectic months. The Zimmerman's, not only of joy at being able to help their friends, but now of gratitude that their home would be well cared for in their absence. And, no, of course they wouldn't accept rent while they were gone—they should be paying their friends for housesitting instead. They talked of travel schedules and the best route to Rochester and the best places to stay and how long they might be there. And as they did, Liz watched big blue eyes fill up and then spill over. Finally, Emma could contain her grief no longer. Turning to bury her face in Frank's chest, she wailed, "Me gonna miss you so much, Unca Fwank!" There was not a dry eye in the group as each of them shared the same prayer: "Please, God, grant that Emmy didn't have to grow up without her beloved Unca Fwank!

Thursday, October 14, 2011

The prayer gatherings had begun spontaneously. The life group Frank and Ginny led had been meeting at their home since the McConnell's home was destroyed. They'd met twice a month for years, but when they learned that a week of testing and research at Mayo had brought Frank no closer to a diagnosis than before, they came, one at a time, to meet around the little pond in the hollow and beseech a loving Father for their friend. And as the first week stretched to two, their Sunday School class joined in. And then their co-workers came, and family after family whose lives had been changed by Zimmerman kindness and hospitality. By the third week, seventy people met, confident their God was hearing how much this quiet man was needed in their lives. By week four, plans were being made to charter a bus. If Frank could not come home to them, they would go to him.

And then the call came. The Zimmerman's were coming home! Whatever had been sucking the life out of this frail, beloved man remained a mystery. Every test at their disposal came back inconclusive. Every doctor they saw eventually admitted defeat. They could not identify the problem. There was nothing they could do. But sometime during that fourth week, a miracle occurred. Frank awakened demanding the biggest breakfast they could bring. He was starving, and besides that, he was tired of just sitting here and being poked and prodded and tested. He thought that going home would be the best medicine they could try, and for the first time in years, he felt his body getting stronger. He knew people had been praying, and he thought his merciful God just might have heard their prayers.

Plans to charter a bus became, instead, plans to throw a welcome-home party. It would be short. The stay at Mayo had been draining. The drive from Rochester to Carthage would be long. Both Frank and Ginny would undoubtedly be exhausted. They would be home tomorrow evening around 6:00, and they would be greeted by balloons and welcome home banners and a month of dinners for the freezer and much love and many, many hugs and prayers. And then they would be left alone to rest. And their good friends the McConnell's, to whom they'd given such faithful encouragement and help the past few months, vowed to give them the same encouragement and help in the days ahead.

17

ALONG a DARK PATH

Midnight
Friday, October 28, 2011
Little Pond in the Hollow

Liz took a deep breath, hungrily drawing in the midnight air. It was unusually warm for the last of October. Normally, she would celebrate any chance to enjoy this garden pond that had been so significant in their lives. Normally, Ethan would be here enjoying it with her.

But not tonight. In fact, not the last few weeks. "What's happened to us, Lord?" she whispered into the dark. "I think our family's falling apart. *I'm* falling apart." Normally, by now she would be looking forward to the holidays, making lists and planning parties and even doing some early Christmas shopping. Of course, this year was anything but normal. It was hard to think of not being in her own home for the season she loved so much. She'd miss the decorating and entertaining and joy of having people in. She thought it was understandable that she would mourn—at least a little—the loss of all the beautiful things she'd collected over the years that she'd dreamed of handing down to her children. But to be honest, she wondered if she could have found the energy or enthusiasm for it, anyway.

She kept trying to remind herself there was so much for which to be thankful. Why couldn't she just hang onto that? By this time next year, they *would* be in their own home. And with their insurance and Ethan's wise planning, it would all be paid for. So why these incessant tears? She was sick of them! They ached in her throat and made her eyes puffy and gave her a headache. No wonder Ethan had become so withdrawn. Who would want to live with a perpetual puddle of tears? But still, she felt so abandoned! He'd always been her rock; the one person in all the world she trusted to love her at her weakest. Well, she was certainly at her weakest now! She needed him, and he wasn't there for her. Or the kids, and she was so worried about the kids. EmmaLeah seemed to have changed overnight from their sunny little princess to the stereotypical "wicked step sister," and it was obvious E.J. was struggling. She could see him watching them both, unspoken questions in those eyes that were much too wise for their years.

She felt anger rising deep in her gut, chasing the tears with breath-taking intensity. It was a vicious cycle now, and it was frightening that she couldn't seem to do a thing about it. She wondered if Ethan felt this same helplessness. More important, she wondered why they couldn't talk about it. Were those walls that were shutting them all out her husband's instinctive response to what he could not control? Was he trying to protect himself and his family from his own anger and hopelessness?

She'd read all the studies on stages of recovery. They both knew all the warnings. They could quote all the statistics and recite the problems common to disaster survivors. In fact, they'd been leading discussion groups on this next, dangerous phase. But teaching concepts was so much easier than living the reality.

She arose from the bench they'd so often shared to pace the cobblestoned path around the pond, remembering her daughter's struggle for her faith along this very trail. But her battle tonight was with no one but herself, and it was one she *would* win. She was determined her family would not be just another statistic, and as angry as she was with her husband right now, she had no doubt he shared that resolve... didn't he?

So, why was she so angry? Why had decisions about the house become so contentious? Certainly there would always be things to disagree about, but they'd always been able to "agreeably disagree" before. Now it seemed that almost every discussion brought tension, if not open conflict. If they didn't get this turned around soon they'd be moving into a beautiful new house full of ugly memories. But disagreements over the house were only a symptom of their real problems, weren't they? She tried to sort out their real problems. This anger that was consuming her very soul certainly topped the list, but was that a cause, or a symptom? How did it relate to her fear for their children and her husband's uncharacteristic reluctance to deal with their issues? It seemed the real problem was that whatever was going on, it had been building for a while and for the first time in their life together they couldn't talk about it. She thought surely what they were going through was not all that uncommon in this storm-haunted community. If only Ethan would agree to some family counseling. The disaster assistance programs they'd attended were helpful, but it was becoming evident they needed something more specific and personal.

Well, she could sit here on this bench in the dark and feel sorry for herself and be mad at her husband—who was probably hurting as much as she was—or she could start figuring things out and looking for solutions.

Her mind went back to the evening she'd first realized there were serious problems. They'd spent most of the day at the construction site and running the countless errands that always seemed to be waiting. Ethan had never voiced any objection to her dream of using the stone from their original entry at their new front door, so she'd assumed the only problem would be whether it could be recovered in a useable form from the neighbor's abandoned yard where it still rested. She'd suggested they stop for coffee to relax a bit and talk about finding someone to move it, and was speechless when he curtly announced he had no intention of going to all the trouble of moving a rock that big when they were paying professionals to build a classy new entry; and besides, he was just too tired to waste time on sentiment when there was so much to think about. She'd recoiled, not only at his harshness, but at the immediate flash of anger that overwhelmed her.

"Back off, Liz," she'd warned herself. He'd been carrying a very heavy load for a long time and he didn't need his wife making it heavier. She knew Ethan, she'd rationalized, and he'd feel badly in the morning. Sometime tomorrow he'd find a way to apologize. She'd tease him about being so grouchy and they'd work things out.

But the next day her husband had been even more distant and unapproachable. He was snowed under, he'd muttered in passing. He'd just grab meals on the run… don't wait up… he'd probably be late.

It was the first night she'd sat alone by the pond—and cried. She turned hopefully as she sensed someone waiting on the bench, then stifled a sigh of disappointment as Ginny said softly, "So what do you plan to do about it, girlfriend?"

"Wh-What? Do about what?"

"Lizzy, Frank and I have watched you sitting alone night after night by this pond. We've seen Ethan pulling away from everyone, even us, and we're concerned. We've been praying for you, but often God's answer is, 'I hear you; now go do something about it.' So Frank plans to catch Ethan on his way out in the morning and take him to breakfast, and here I am. Please forgive us if we're meddling, but we love you guys and we can't just sit back and watch you self-destruct."

Relief flooded through Liz. For the first time in weeks she wasn't alone. She settled onto the bench, encouraged by her good friend's candor. "We can't fix this by ourselves, Ginny. I think neither of us has any idea what's wrong. We need counseling and the kids need it, too, but I can't get Ethan to even talk about it. So, I guess Monday I'll call the church and get a recommendation for a good family therapist for the kids and me. And I really need you to pray for me. This anger I'm fighting all the time is really wearing me down."

10:00 p.m.
Saturday, October 29, 2011

Liz knew running here now was definitely a bad idea. Even though the path around her little pond was familiar territory, it was one of those nights so dark the eye cannot adjust. There was no moon, and stars crowding the canopy above delivered little more than glittering ornaments for an inky sky. A reckless fall would certainly not be honoring her vow to keep her body healthy after the miraculous healing of her legs, but sitting still was not an option. She had to run. The anguish of another lonely, silent day pursued her, propelling her over the stones… round and round… on and on… faster and faster… until

125

finally the urgency of lungs desperate for air defeated all other demands. She staggered to a stop by the bench, hands on her knees, gasping for breath.

"Liz."

She jumped at the barely audible voice of her husband. He sat unmoving, inches from where she'd stopped, a shadow in the deep night.

"Ethan...?" The voice out of the dark had been taut, unreadable. She waited, unwilling to risk her fragile spirit to uncertain hope. A slight rustle alerted her to the hand he extended. She laid her own lightly in his upturned palm and cautiously allowed him to guide her to the bench beside him. They sat in silence, hand in hand, shoulder to shoulder; yet, her heart mourned, still so far apart.

A sliver of moon began its circuit over the hollow. She darted a glance at the silent face beside her and felt her heart sink. He seemed as distant as ever, eyes fixed on something she could not discern.

Then he turned to her and in the dim light she saw eyes dulled with pain, tears coursing unheeded down his face. He whispered brokenly, "I can't stop thinking about them, Liz. They're always with me. No one should have to suffer what they did, or see what we did. There were souls hollowed out by horror that night, and I can't shut them out of my mind. I keep hearing the ones we couldn't reach in time, trapped and hurting and screaming for help. And every time I get in the car I see that woman clutching her little bleeding baby, so horribly maimed I can't imagine it survived. I'm afraid to go to sleep because I dream that mutilated child in the front seat is ours and the mother in such agony is you! How can I worry about floor finishes and paint and the latest gadgets and patio stones when that poor mother's eyes keep haunting me?"

Liz was stunned, and suddenly ashamed. "Oh, Ethan! I'm so sorry! I should have realized... I should have been more tuned in to your needs... I've just been so overwhelmed with my own anger and sadness. I can't make sense of it, and I've been so afraid for us. It seems like we've been growing farther and farther apart when we need each other the most and I haven't had a clue what to do. Maybe I was trying to make that stupid rock some sort of 'stone of remembrance'… some connection with the life we had before. Ethan, we don't have to build the house. We can sell the property and find a place to buy, or even rent. It isn't worth what you're going through…"

He pulled her close then, holding her fiercely. "It isn't the house, Elizabeth, and it certainly isn't you. I know I haven't been there for you and the kids, but I've been petrified that if I let myself feel anything I'd fly in a million pieces and never find them all again. I can't stop thinking that I almost lost all of you and I couldn't do a thing about it. I should believe God is in control, but instead I feel like everything is out of control and I don't know how to deal with it. I never imagined I'd be where I am now…"

She drew back to take his face in her hands, forcing him to look at her. "Ethan, I decided last night that I'd call the church Monday and find a family counselor for the kids and me. They're out of control, too. I don't know how to help them through this time, and it's obvious I'm not even going to be able to fix me without help." She looked down, afraid she might not hear the answer she knew they needed. "Honey, I know it's hard for the counselor to seek counseling, but… will you come with us?"

He pulled her back against him and sat, holding her so tightly, so long, that she began to be afraid. She resisted the impulse to ask him to let go… to plead, "Well…?" It was so good to be close again; she didn't want to break the spell, but…

Finally, he relaxed his hold and said with a forced laugh, "I have to admit, I am one wise man to marry up so high. I'll make the calls first thing Monday."

She pivoted to pull his arm around her shoulders, grateful to be together in this place. They lingered there, calmed by the music of the night; comforted by the silence of hearts that once again needed no spoken language. Finally, they knelt before the bench that now became their altar, offering up battle-weary spirits to their waiting Father, grateful that He knew their every need.

And up the hill, in a darkened bedroom that overlooked their garden sanctuary, friends who loved them well enough to wait with them knelt, lifting up their names before His throne.

Liz was the first to break the silence. "Well, My Love, I know the safest place to be is on our knees, but these war-weary knees are shouting at me, so…"

Ethan remorsefully rose to help her to her feet and suddenly found himself inundated with visions of that terrible night six months ago—a sinister tsunami that left him breathless and reeling. He saw his wife sitting quietly on the curb of their shattered life, concerned only that her family was safe, and her calm confession she could not walk still echoed through his very soul. What good had come of all her suffering? Then his mind's eye saw his only son stumble out of that ominous cloud of dust and debris, and he wondered if he'd ever be able to forgive himself for leaving them alone. He should have been there to protect them. He should have been his wife's strength; not weak and helpless in the face of all she'd endured. Now he'd let his weakness multiply her pain. Why had he just waited here on this bench! What if that pounding run had rekindled the paralysis she'd worked so hard to conquer? He should have stopped her! How could he ever live with himself if…

"It's OK, Honey. I'm just stiff from not cooling down after such an intense run. I'm gonna be sore tomorrow for sure, but my legs are fine and Gramma's cane is definitely relegated back to dog discourager again, at least until I'm ninety-four. I know you think you should have somehow sheltered us all from the storm and I love you for it, but we both know we were exactly where God placed us that day, and we just have to accept we may never know why. Now stop beating yourself up and *please* give me a hand!"

This time his laugh was anything but forced. "I don't know how you do it, Babe, but I have to admit it's a relief to have you reading my mind again. Just have to remember to keep it clean!" he added theatrically. "Do you feel like sitting here a little longer? We have some catching up to do."

Somehow a corner had been turned. They still had a lot of work to do, but somehow, in some way, this garden path would lead them out of the dark place that had threatened to destroy their family.

They settled close again, drinking in the liquid tranquility of the dawn. The silver crescent yawned its satisfaction for a job well done and spilled its luminescence into day. Companion jewels took the cue and winked out one by one. Still they lingered.

And up the hill, a dawn-kissed patio overlooked their garden refuge, and friends who loved them well enough to watch with them lifted up their thanks before God's throne.

18

THANKSGIVING DAY
and OTHER SWEET SURPRISES

9:00 p.m.
Thursday, November 24, 2011

Thanksgiving Day had been such a sweet surprise! Liz sat in their darkened living room reliving each moment, enjoying the happy sounds of children's chatter as E.J. and Emma helped Dad and Uncle Frank and Aunt Ginny clean up "so Mommy can rest." She was doing just that, relishing this quiet time alone, drawing the peacefulness of the evening around her tired spirit.

She hadn't wanted to admit how much she'd been dreading the holiday season; especially Thanksgiving. Her passion for this uniquely American holiday had begun when she was just a tiny girl. She'd loved sitting on her mother's kitchen counter, "helping" her stuff the turkey and peel potatoes; watching the timer for just the right time to take the pies out of the oven; trying to wait patiently for that exciting moment when she would be allowed to carefully take Gramma's china out of the antique cabinet one piece at a time and place it just so on the dining room table. Later, as the mother of her own tiny girls, she'd marveled at Beth O'Leary's patience (and courage) as little hands had "helped" set her own table with that same delicate china. Her delight in the day had grown as her family had grown, and each year since they'd moved into their brick-and-stone dwelling in southwest Joplin, Liz had reveled in the joyful chaos of three generations coming together around their massive dining table to eat and laugh and give thanks and argue about football.

But this year, as November came she'd struggled to feel thankful... to accept that their beloved table was gone... that their precious heritage china would never again welcome a family celebration... that in this year of the tornado she would host no happy chaos and laughter and arguments around any table... that for the first time their family would be scattered.

The first, unexpected call from her parents had surprised her. The O'Leary's would be staying in northern Missouri to be with the Anderson's this year. Tom was doing well, but Teona, always a bit fragile, seemed never to have quite recovered from their terrifying flight down what she called "the stairway to hell." Liz admired her parents' compassionate hearts, and she didn't doubt their friends were their primary reason for staying home. But the unspoken truth was that Big Mike was still fighting to regain his normal vigor, and Liz thought the idea of two trips to Joplin within a month just might be more than he could handle. Well, at least they'd be here for Christmas, when Elly was home.

But Elly would not be home for Thanksgiving! Though that call had not surprised her, Lizzy's heart had still sunk when it came. If the thought of her cherished day of thanks without her parents had been painful, the certainty that her first-born child would be somewhere else had been almost intolerable. Liz shook her head. In spite of all their prayers, Elly just could not let go of the guilt she carried for her best friend's unremitting pain. It was becoming more and more probable that Ali could be facing reconstructive surgery soon, so it was not surprising that Elly would feel she should be with her during the short Thanksgiving break. But Liz couldn't help but wonder if, buried somewhere in her daughter's tender heart, there might not be the same dread her own heart felt at the prospect of Thanksgiving without their family's cherished traditions. As usual, Ethan had seen right through her forced cheerfulness. She'd been relieved, and then grateful when he'd insisted she confront her heartache with a whole new set of traditions. Maybe they couldn't bring others to their table this year, but they could take their "table" to others. They would begin by delivering food to families at "FEMA Village" and then they would serve lunch to the homeless at Outreach House. By last night she was beginning to share the Little's enthusiasm for "helping all those people tomorrow."

Then, just as she was putting two very excited children to bed, Frank and Ginny had appeared at their patio door and this most unprecedented Thanksgiving had become even more unusual. The Zimmerman's were hosting five "tornado families" for dinner tomorrow evening and they'd just heard Elly and the O'Leary's wouldn't be home. Sorry—if they'd known sooner, they wouldn't have waited so late. They knew what it was like to long for family during the holidays, and they'd already set four more places for Ethan and Liz and their little buddies. No, they would not take "no" for an answer, and no, Liz did not need to bring a thing. It was just that family needed to be together, and since they were family at heart, well...

So once again, Liz had awakened this morning to a strange new world. By the time they'd finished their deliveries to the second unit at FEMA Village, her heart was singing. It had seemed such a small thing—just a cardboard box with a smoked turkey and Thanksgiving dinner prepared by people of area churches and charities. But most of these families were still struggling. Many were still without work in lieu of jobs that would not return until restaurants and stores and small businesses had been rebuilt, if ever. Some still wondered if they'd ever be able to work again... if they would ever fully recover from their injuries. And most still had no idea where they'd be living a year from now, or even two.

As they'd worked their way through their assigned row of temporary homes, E.J. and Emma had become more and more excited at the hugs and smiles and grateful "thank yous" they were getting. And then it had happened. The big, burly man had opened the door and frowned as Ethan explained they represented area neighbors who wanted to wish them a "Happy Thanksgiving." He hadn't said a word, just stared at the box as his face colored a deep, angry red; then slammed the door in their faces. Tender-hearted Emma had immediately burst into tears, but as their mother tried to comfort her, E.J. had whispered urgently, "Dad. We have to leave it here. I saw little kids in there and every kid has to have turkey for Thanksgiving. I bet after we leave they'll come and get it." His parents had shared a look of approval over his head. They would leave it! They had set the box carefully against the door, praying the needs of the children in that home would overcome this wounded man's pride. Ethan had made a note of the trailer number. He would try to come back here in a few days. Surely out of his own trauma from the tornado he could find a way to connect.

In the heart of downtown Joplin just a few blocks from the tornado's path, Outreach House had proven a stranger world yet. Liz knew some of her friends at church routinely volunteered there, serving lunches or processing donations. She'd often dropped off contributions of clothing or household supplies, and even sometimes thought it might be good for the kids to help in a charity like this. But their lives were so busy, and since the agency was a homeless shelter, some of the men seen hanging out there seemed a little scary, so…

Now designated as a temporary disaster shelter, the small old brick building's three floors were a beehive of activity. Beds still neatly lined all but the main floor. Staff cheerfully kept order, overseeing volunteers who came to welcome refugees and serve meals and catalog donations of food and supplies that still poured in. But this was no stereotypically dreary "soup kitchen." Bedding was clean and fresh. The well-equipped kitchen was spotless and up to code. Walls were recently painted a cheerful creamy white, and fall decorations graced long tables that were immediately cleared and cleaned as new "customers" appeared, plates loaded with traditional Thanksgiving fare.

Liz had guardedly positioned her children on either side of her behind one of the long serving tables, and quickly found herself humbled by their joyful proffer of friendship with every serving of mashed potatoes. She'd watched with pride (and no small measure of contrition) as haggard faces and tired eyes brightened at her children's welcoming smiles and cheerful chatter, and she'd nodded a grateful assent when E.J. had excitedly asked, "Mom, can we come back and help real soon?

The families around the Zimmerman tables this evening had been a fascinatingly eclectic gathering. Liz was beginning to see that the wind that had blown away her house had also blown away a world that had been far too safe and comfortable. It was a chastening realization. If this was the first time in her life she'd actually shared an intimate evening with people of such varying color and background, or spent her most-treasured holiday with strangers in need, her horizons were definitely much too narrow. What was it old Shakespeare said? "It is an ill wind that blows nobody any good…"

This morning her heart had longed for happier times, when this day would have seen her family gathered around the colossal table with which Ethan had surprised her on their fifth wedding anniversary. She smiled wistfully, remembering his excitement on that long-ago day. He loved this time of year every bit as much as she and they both had loved that table that symbolized so much. Ethan James McConnell II, of all people, knew how suddenly and irrevocably precious family time together could be lost.

Now she knew those family times would come again. Someday soon another big table would see her family gathered to eat and laugh and give thanks and argue about football. But when it did her heart would not be the same. This evening she sat, wrapped in grateful memories of a most unexpected day, knowing that when the time for which they longed finally came again, "family" would always include strangers in need and "FEMA Village people."

10:00 p.m.
Northern Missouri

Beth O'Leary watched her husband's reflection in the kitchen window as she quietly finished putting away the last of the dishes. She'd loved this big man through more joys and sorrows than one could count, and now her heart ached as he sat dozing in his favorite chair, still much weaker than he should have been at this stage of recovery.

"Please, Lord!" She didn't even try to quiet her heart's plea, or voice her appeal for healing. She knew her caring Father heard. Surely the God they served still had work for them to do. Desperate souls still needed her big farmer's touch. Their family still needed his wise counsel. And she would always need her husband's joyful strength. She struggled to suppress the sob that threatened to escape. She knew what Mike would say: "No tears, Mary Elizabeth!"

Then she smiled, remembering their conversation this morning at breakfast. "We have no right to demand even one more minute from God," her husband had asserted. "He's been so good to us, and His plan is always right. We have to trust Him now." Then he'd added with that twinkle in green eyes she still adored, "But that doesn't mean you should give up on us yet, and don't you dare stop praying!"

Well, no worries about that! He knew she'd never stop praying. Often it was the only thing that got her through.

She jumped. "Mike, how did you...!" He was standing behind her, hands on either side of her on the counter, grinning over her shoulder at their reflections in the glass. How such a big man could move so quietly never failed to amaze her. She allowed him to lead her into the living room and waited until he was ready to talk.

"Tom's worried about Teona, Beth. He says she's hardly sleeping, and if she does she has nightmares. He's tried to talk her into getting help, but..."

"She told me, Mike. But I couldn't get her to listen to me, either."

Big Michael Patrick O'Leary and Thomas Vincent Anderson had been friends since high school. They'd followed different paths after college; Tom to the Marines and Mike to the ranch his family had owned for several generations. But they'd always stayed in touch, and when Tom had come home with a beautiful black-eyed bride from Kenya, they'd simply taken up where they'd left off.

Mary Elizabeth McCray O'Leary and Teona Makena Njenga Anderson had quickly become friends as well, sharing lunches and shopping trips and hopes for houses full of babies. And when, after Lizzy was born, first Beth and then Teona had faced the bitter disappointment that there would be no more babies, they'd cried together and prayed together and then decided they were blessed to have the families God had given them, and they would make that be enough.

Now Teona's once-lustrous, velvety-black skin was grey with fatigue, her slight frame so thin her usually-elegant clothes hung limply from her shoulders. Since they'd returned from Joplin six months ago Tom had flourished, but his wife had seemed to wither before their eyes.

Well, Beth had let her only daughter face this sad Thanksgiving without her because a good friend needed help, and she wasn't about to let her just give up and die. Tomorrow they would find a counselor who could help, and Beth would be by Teona's side until she was well. And as for Big Mike, she would just keep praying, and believe God's promises.

19

From VICTIM to VICTOR—SOMEDAY

9:00 a.m.
Thursday, December 15, 2011
McConnell Basement Apartment

Liz thought she really should get started decorating. For the first time she could remember, she was having a hard time even thinking about it; but it had been important to Ginny, so she'd better see if she couldn't generate some enthusiasm. Ginny had made it very clear she and Frank expected a big celebration when they returned in late December and they certainly owed them that.

The Zimmerman's had decided to spend the Christmas season shuttling between their parents' homes in New England. Ginny had confided on the drive to the Tulsa airport yesterday that since the tornado they'd felt an urgency to be with them more. Their parents were all in good health, thank God, but when they thought of how life could change in an instant... well, they didn't want to wake up some day and wish they'd paid more attention to their families.

It really was true, Liz thought, they were all tornado survivors. Whether one's address was Joplin, MO, or one of the smaller towns surrounding the city, no one had been untouched. She liked the sign she'd seen yesterday at one of the little independent relief centers that dotted the area: "Distribution Center for Tornado Victors." Maybe someday she'd write a book, "From Victim to Victor, One Family's Journey." She was looking forward to the day they could claim that title. But for now, there were still days it was so tempting to crawl back into that dark hiding place her battered spirit had found. It was amazing how much energy it still sometimes took to simply put one foot in front of the other, and this seemed to be one of those days.

Maybe it was because the house was so silent. She'd never noticed before how reassuring it had become just knowing Frank and Ginny were there. Their quiet strength and generosity had become a lifeline for all of them. She had no idea how Ginny had managed it, but they'd come home from the airport to find a note on the patio door: "Please reconsider the possibility of moving upstairs while we're gone. You know how warm and cozy the house is when it's decorated, and I just can't bear the thought of such dear friends spending the holidays in a dreary basement, especially after all you've been through. I've moved our decorations from the storage shed into the back hall in hopes you'll feel like using some of them—makes me sad to think of them just sitting there. At the least, please take whatever you need to decorate downstairs. It would make me feel so much better, and I'm really looking forward to seeing what you've done with them when we get back."

Liz had to laugh. Their basement home was hardly "dreary." Shortly after they were married, the Zimmerman's had sorrowfully confronted their truth. Frank's health problems meant there would be no little Zimmerman's unless they chose to adopt. But since his hold on life would always be tenuous at best, they decided instead to make their home a refuge for children who needed help. That passion to extend help had expanded to college students and families in crisis, and when they'd purchased property in a rural area just outside Carthage a few years ago, they'd designed their new house with a beautifully decorated and furnished "house under a house" so they could live out that vision. Liz had no idea how many had enjoyed the peace and comfort of this retreat in the country, but she knew there was almost always someone staying here.

"Well, Elizabeth," she muttered. "Time to suck it up and make this Christmas as magic as possible for two little McConnell's who need something beautiful in their lives." She'd bring some of Ginny's boxes down and the kids could help go through them this evening. Maybe they'd even drag that tree out that she'd seen in the back storage area.

10:30 p.m.

Christmas Eve, 2011

Elly sat motionless, listening. She was certain she'd heard Mom and Dad close their door a few minutes ago. They always went to bed fairly early on Christmas Eve so they could get up extra early Christmas morning. "After all," her mom had once winked, "Santa occasionally needs a little help and we want to be there if he does." She'd been strangely comforted that at least this little tradition seemed to have survived. But now…

She was sure she'd heard a little strangled sob. She'd just finished her journal entry, wearily looking forward to the soft, warm comforter that always welcomed her to this cheerful little basement room. A rush of gratitude swept over her. Ginny had gone to so much trouble to try to give her some sense of "home" in this temporary place of refuge. Elly wondered how many stores and websites and catalogs she'd visited to find bedding so much like her room in Joplin.

She crept into the hall, listening intently. That quiet little sob had sounded like it was coming from the Little's room. Were one of them having another nightmare? Since that night on the patio they'd both seemed so much more at peace than the rest of the family, but she'd read that it wasn't unusual for disaster survivors to regress several times before they worked their way through all the trauma. Certainly she and Ali still had a long way to go.

There it was again! She whirled at the presence of someone in the living room. There in the dim light of the twinkling tree sat her brother, curled tightly into a ball in the corner, arms around his knees in an eerie reprise of her own ritual of self-sanctuary.

"E.J.?"

He didn't respond. Just looked at her, tears slipping silently down his face.

She moved to slide delicately down beside him, gently slipping her arm around his shoulders.

He turned then, dissolving into her arms, sobbing as though his heart would break; in his grief reverting back to "little boy" status.

"Oh, Sissy, I tried not to be sad. I really do like it here. Me and Mom and Emmy had a great time decorating and I think it looks really

139

good, don't you? Bu—but—but I—I miss my room and my tree house and I wanna g-go-o-o h-ho-m-m-m-e! I don't wanna get up on Christmas somewhere eh–el-l-l-ls-s-se!"

Elly's heart broke for her little brother—and for herself. As a matter of fact, she didn't want to either! Wordlessly she pulled him into her lap and they sat cuddled together, mourning their losses, comforting each other with their tears.

Without thinking, she began humming his "God-song." How he'd loved to hear her sing "his special God-song" about how much Jesus loves Ethan James McConnell III when he was a toddler. When had they stopped? How had that happened? Well, he needed it now, so once again she softly sang the song she'd made up for him, and as she sang she felt her brother—who was, after all, still just a little boy—slowly relax in her arms. He slept, and still she sat, holding him close. Then she slept; and her father found them there beside the glimmering tree on Christmas morning; "the sweetest Christmas present of all," he'd thought, "except for Jesus Christ Himself!!

20

SERIOUSLY SEEKING "NORMAL"

2:00 p.m.
Wednesday, January 4, 2012
Highway 69

Christmas had been strange this year. No real surprise there, Elly thought. There wasn't much that wasn't strange. She felt a little sad at how relieved she was to be headed back to school; and more than a little guilty. Most of Joplin didn't have the luxury of just retreating to a more comfortable place. What was it her grandfather had said last summer? "The best thing you can do for this family is go to school and have a good time and do all the things an eighteen-year-old girl should do."

"OK, Big Pops," she muttered, "How do I have a good time when my little brother and sister still don't have a home! I know, technically I don't have a home either, but right now at least my life has some degree of normalcy at school. So tell me what to do with this feeling that I've completely deserted them when things are really hard." Unexpected tears blurred the road and she quickly swung her car toward the little roadside park just ahead. "I wish I could sit down and have a long talk with you, Poppy. What would you tell me now?"

As if on cue, she heard that gruff voice she adored, drilling into her spirit once again one of the most important lessons she'd ever need to learn: "...don't feel like you have to be God!" She smiled through her tears, picturing green eyes that could pierce to the bone. "He's perfectly capable of taking care of your family while you're gone."

Maybe she'd been expecting too much. She'd been surprised how much the home-sickness had grown as the holidays approached. She'd warned herself over and over that so many of the things she loved about Christmas just wouldn't be there this year. Her mom was pretty incredible, but even she couldn't decorate and entertain and create the kind of magic they were used to when everything they had was gone. But, she'd rationalized, they'd all be together, and wasn't that what it was all about anyway?

The problem was, it had felt like a whole different family she'd come home to. They'd all been waiting there to welcome her; even Big Pops and Gran, but under all the smiles and hugs and welcome homes there was a vague sense of unrest. Mom and Dad had seemed more attentive to each other than ever. The Little's tagged her around, competing for her attention as always. The apartment had been surprisingly festive, thanks to Ginny's decorations and Mom's creativity and, according to her little brother and sister, all their help. She smiled again, remembering their excitement at showing her every little detail of every decoration in the place. But still, there was that indefinable something that had worried her, especially after her little brother's melt-down Christmas Eve.

Maybe, she'd thought, it was because Frank and Ginny were gone. They'd become such a strengthening force in their lives. She was sorry she had to leave before they got home, but she certainly agreed they needed to spend as much time as possible with their families before they came back to Missouri.

And she felt she'd hardly seen Gran and Pops. They'd been there such a short time, partly because it was still hard to find a place to stay; but mostly, Elly thought, because Pops' recovery was going much more slowly than they'd hoped. He'd seemed so quiet—not at all the dynamic force that filled the room she'd always relished. She was trying not to worry, but she couldn't deny a nagging sense of fear that they still might lose him. "Please, Pops. Please get well" she silently pleaded. "We need you so much!"

She was relieved, and admittedly a little apprehensive, when the day after her grandparents left her parents called a family meeting. They knew she was doing well academically—good for her—but how was she doing otherwise? Any physical repercussions from the tornado? Any anger or fear issues? Any PTSD symptoms? How was she doing emotionally and spiritually?

She'd told them about the pact she and Ali had made to be open with each other about their struggles, and how myriad midnight calls were helping them through the nightmares that seemed to pursue so many tornado survivors. Otherwise, she thought she was doing pretty well. She was so glad her journal was a tornado survivor, too, and that Dad had taught her to journal when she was little. It was really cathartic to write down her feelings. Yes, she'd found a church she liked and was making friends there, but she missed the girls she'd been mentoring a lot. She stayed in touch as much as she could find time, but it was definitely not the same kind of relationship. She was hoping next semester she could form a new group through the church there. Just seemed to be something she really needed, and she liked to think she'd been a positive influence on girls who didn't have much positive in their lives.

So now… what weren't they telling her?

She'd seen her mother's grin, and knew exactly what she was thinking. "So much like her grandfather!" That's OK. She couldn't think of a better role model.

"Well, Mike, Jr.," her father had teased, "that's one of the reasons for this meeting. Your mom and I realized we weren't doing very well with some of our memories, so we've been taking advantage of the disaster relief counseling they've been offering. E.J. and Emmy are going, too, aren't you, Kiddos? Is there anything you want to tell your big sister about what you're learning?"

Always the leader, E.J. had proclaimed, "I didn't want to talk, but Mr. Chris is really nice, and I'm glad Dad made us go. Besides," solemn brown eyes had turned suddenly merry again, "we usually get ice cream after."

While E.J had been talking, Emma had slipped quietly onto Elly's lap, twirling her sister's long black hair around her finger, as she had since she was a baby. "We get to go see him again tomorrow, Sissy. Will you go wif us?"

She was so glad Emma hadn't lost that last endearing little lisp! She'd planted a quick kiss on top of her sister's red curls and looked a question at her father.

"It's been a real help to us as a family, El. We know you don't want to spend what little time you have at home reliving all you went through, but I think it would be a good thing for all of us if you could come. What do you think?"

It *had* been helpful, Elly thought. Painful, but helpful. It had been hard to hear her parents confessing their struggles. In her eyes they'd always been invincible, and they'd both been such rocks since the tornado. But, as Chris the Counselor had said, rocks have a hard time being flexible, and in this environment, survival demands flexibility. So, somehow he'd brought her face to face with her own inflexibility and made her confront issues she hadn't realized she'd buried. Could that be why she felt like running back to a "safer" environment? Was she running from weaknesses she didn't want to see in her parents, or in herself?

She'd met with him one more time alone, and he'd given her the name of a woman near the college she could trust. She thought she'd probably give her a call, maybe even encourage Ali to talk to the woman near her whose name Chris had also given her.

It would be good to see Ali again. She was grateful for Mom and Dad's unselfishness. She knew they'd have loved to keep her home longer, but they understood how important time with her friend was. They'd all been disappointed Ali wasn't able to come down during the Christmas break, but she'd had doctors' appointments she couldn't miss. Elly couldn't think of her without a sinking feeling in her stomach. Her arm had gotten even worse. She was in so much pain, and the latest MRI had shown it wasn't healing straight. When she'd left the Wilson home after Thanksgiving, they'd still felt there was hope Ali's arm might heal; but there was very little question now it would require more surgery soon. As usual, Ali had taken it in stride, but Elly was having a real problem with the idea that her friend would have to go through even more trauma.

She hoped the counselor Chris recommended so highly would be able to help her work through the guilt she still carried. She supposed that was why there was a little uneasiness as she got closer to Ft. Scott. If she'd just discovered feelings she'd buried, what might she see in her friend's eyes? What might be lost in their relationship because of all this?

She shook her head. It was amazing how deep the wounds were from that monster that still haunted all of them, and it seemed that no matter how much you thought you trusted the Lord; there was still a lot of stuff to wade through.

3:00 a.m.
Thursday, January 5, 2012
Wilson Home

Elly came awake with a start. She thought she'd heard a moan, and it sounded 'way too much like that horrible moment last May when she'd found her friend trapped under that huge piece of metal. Had something happened to Ali? Was she having another of those terrifying nightmares? She lay still, listening. All she could hear was Ali's even breathing. Well. Maybe it was her own dream that woke her. She checked her phone. Three o'clock—good! She could get in at least three or four more hours' sleep before Ali's mom would have breakfast ready. She sighed and pulled the covers up to her chin, burrowing deep into the featherbed she'd slept in for years. She smiled, remembering a twelve-year-old Ali excitedly ushering her into "their" new bedroom in the Wilson's just-remodeled house in Joplin, urging her to try out "her" new featherbed. She hadn't known what to say. She remembered thinking Ali's folks must have really meant it when they said she was part of the family. So much had happened since then. How many hours had they spent in that cheerful room; laughing, crying, sharing dreams and heartaches, even arguing... but always together. Strange. That house hadn't even been touched by the storm. But Ali...

She yawned, willing tense muscles to relax, allowing tired eyes to close. But then, just as she began to drift off again, Ali's voice rang out.

"Big Michael! Wait. Please... I need to ask you something. Please don't leave. Please! No..."

Elly fumbled for the bedside lamp and quickly moved across the room. A chill ran down her spine. Alison was sitting rigidly upright, eyes wide in that fixed stare reminiscent of their drive home from Kansas City last August. Her heart ached for her friend. She knew only too well how painful these unrelenting nightmares were; how exhausted they never failed to leave one afterward.

But there was something different this time. Instead of fear in those wide brown eyes, Elly saw… what? …pleading? …and tears! Well, she couldn't let her friend suffer. She perched lightly on the edge of Ali's bed, gently shaking her shoulder.

"Ali. Ali, you're dreaming. Al."

"No! Don't!" Eyes still unseeing, Ali shook her head and brushed at Elly's hand on her shoulder. "No-o-o-o! He's leaving! Please come back! Mi-i-i-chael-l-l-l…!"

"Ali! It's just a dream! Please, wake up."

Finally! She saw consciousness slowly return as Ali turned wistful eyes to her.

"Elly. He was here! It wasn't just a dream. It was Big Michael. I could feel his hand on my head and he talked to me…" She breathed a long sigh and stared into the shadowy room.

Elly sat, forcing herself to be patient. What should she do now? Was this one of those emotional breakdowns the counselors had warned of? Ali had seemed fine when they went to bed; actually much more reconciled about her arm than Elly had managed to be…

Suddenly her friend turned what could only be described as "radiant" eyes to her. "Elly, he promised the nightmares would be better now! He said we need dreams to help us sort out our fears and feelings, and we're doing the right thing talking to each other. But he said nightmares aren't healthy dreams, and we're going to be healed… he actually used that word… he promised we're already being healed right now, and by summer they'll all be gone. Isn't that amazing? I feel like a huge weight has just been lifted off my shoulders."

Elly sat open-mouthed, trying to take it all in. Far be it from her to question whether it could be true. This past year she'd seen so many things that weren't logical that were real. But still…

"Ouch! Ali!" She was shocked out of her reverie at Ali's white-knuckled grip on her arm.

Her usually compassionate friend didn't even seem to notice.

"El, I just remembered! There was a huge butterfly! When I was loading the car to leave for your house that Sunday, there was an enormous butterfly just sitting on the rosebush right by my car door. I don't know why I didn't think it was strange. I've never seen such a gigantic one before, and why would a butterfly want to be there? That bush is dead! Do you think…?"

"I don't know, Al. I know Mom and I saw those three huge butterflies at the window the day of the tornado, and "Big Michael's" wings looked just like one of them. I guess if they really were angels, it wouldn't be any problem for one of them to get from here to Joplin."

"He gave me a message for you, Elly."

"Who? Big Michael? When?"

"Just a few minutes ago. He said to tell you it wasn't your fault."

"Seriously!" For some reason, Elly suddenly felt defensive. She was s-o-o tired of everyone telling her that! "If he had a message for me, why didn't he tell me himself? What wasn't my fault? Are you sure you weren't dreaming?"

Ali shrugged and looked down at her cast, white in the dim light. "He said you have to stop feeling guilty. You have to…" She faltered, evading her friend's questioning gaze.

"C'mon, Al. I know that look! So what did your big 'angel' say about me?"

Her friend's eyes came up at that, and Elly was immediately ashamed of her snarky tone. "I'm so sorry, Al! That sounded just like Emmy when E.J. got to talk to his "butterfly guy" and she didn't! No wonder he didn't want to talk to me!"

"Oh, Elly! I'm sure it wasn't that! I don't know why he wanted me to play go-between. I certainly don't like the idea; but I do know this: When he said your name, it was like this amazing love just washed over both of us! That's how I know the nightmares are going away. And why I have to tell you…" She paused again, then blurted, "He said to tell you, 'There's only one God and you have to stop trying to be Him.'"

Elly stared at her in shock as her friend stared back, tears gathering behind long blond lashes. Then it was Alison's turn to wonder about a possible melt-down. Suddenly Elly was doubled over, laughing almost hysterically.

Finally, she caught her breath enough to speak. "Ali, that's exactly what Mom and Dad and Big Pops all said. Ya think Someone even bigger is trying to tell me something? I must have a lot worse problem than I thought."

4:00 a.m.

Elly sighed into the quiet room. She was so tired, and Ali hadn't moved since they'd said that quick prayer for each other and turned out the light. If she could just get her brain to stop spinning, hopefully they'd be able to sleep in as long as they wished this morning...

The voice was surprisingly serene in the darkness. "My surgery's scheduled for next month, El."

Now it was Elly's turn to sit straight up in bed. "What?! When? Where? Why didn't you tell me sooner? Are you..."

Ali's soft giggle stopped her. "It's OK, El. I'm really looking forward to getting it done. The doctors say they can fix everything, and I'm just ready to do whatever it takes to move on. It's in KC February 17th. That's a Thursday, so I was hoping maybe you could drive up Saturday when I come home."

"Seriously? I'll be waiting at the hospital when you wake up on Thursday. And that's a promise!"

5:00 p.m.
Thursday, February 17, 2012
Kansas City, MO

Elly rushed breathlessly into the surgery waiting room. "How is she, Wil? I thought she'd be in recovery by now."

She had wanted so much to be at the hospital before Ali went in for this all-important reconstruction on her arm, but her test today was an absolute "must," so she'd left immediately after class, determined to at least get here before Ali came out of recovery.

"She'll probably be there another hour or so, Elly. It's OK," he quickly reassured at her look of panic. "They delayed the surgery. Dr. Landro called. He heard Ali was having problems and came up from Houston to do the reconstruction. Can you imagine? He insists he's not even turning in charges. Says she shouldn't be having to go through all this and wants to take care of her. I knew he'd really been touched by what was going on in Joplin, but now I'm thinking he must have taken a personal interest in Ali's case. They say he'd left orders to send him regular updates. That's how he knew..."

"Elly! You made it! I'm so glad." Elly relaxed into Helen Wilson's warm embrace, briefly reflecting how many times this woman's gentle hugs had comforted her since she was a little girl. "It will help Ali so much to see you when she wakes up, and frankly, you're an encouragement to Wil and me, too. We got you an adjoining room at the hotel. You can just ride back and forth with us while you're here."

"Oh, thanks, Helen, but I want to be here at the hospital as much as I can. I'll just sleep in the waiting room."

"Nonsense! I appreciate your loyalty, Dear Heart, but you'll need a place to shower and get a little sleep, or we'll end up having to visit *two* daughters in the hospital. Now, it's going to be a while before we hear anything, so let's get a cup of that terrible coffee and hear all about you and your family. How's Big Mike?"

"Mr. and Mrs. Wilson? And... Elly, right?" If they'd been impressed with this busy surgeon's caring heart before, the fact that he'd remembered Elly's name elevated him to the very top of their lists. "She's in recovery. You can see her in a minute. We're in pretty good shape, now. If she's as courageous about rehab as she's been up to now, in a year her arm should be pretty much back to normal. She'll always have the scars, of course, but we managed to minimize those and I'll put her on an exercise regimen that will build her muscles back to the size they should be, so don't be discouraged by what you see at first. I'm so sorry she's had to go through this added pain and trauma. That bone should not have slipped like it did, but, well, it won't happen again. I know you want to be with her now, but when she's awake and ready, we'll go over what we did and what she can expect for the future. She should be able to go home in a couple days."

10:00 p.m.
Monday, February 22, 2012

The drive back from Ft. Scott had been so, so different from the drive to Kansas City! It felt like a thousand pounds had been lifted from her heart. Elly thought for the first time in months she could go to bed and know she would sleep well.

Ali was home, and talking to the physical therapist who would be taking over her case there in Ft. Scott. When Dr. Landro had shown them her x-rays, it had been so reassuring to see that nice, straight arm. But they'd all been shocked at the "before" one—no wonder she'd been in such pain! Well, it was all behind them now, and her irrepressible friend already had a huge smiley face calendar on her wall with target dates marked in red, like, "CAST OFF" and "SWIM" and "DRIVE!!!" She'd be back in school by next week, and planned to spend the rest of this one catching up. The college had been so good to work with her. It still seemed people in this region just couldn't do enough to help tornado survivors, and Elly was more than grateful.

21

The REST of the PROMISE

6:30 a.m.
Monday, March 19, 2012

"OK, Mr. Mysterious. What have you been up to now? I know you've been planning something. I've seen that look too many times."

Ethan just grinned and turned toward Range Line. They were both volunteering at the church later today, but first they'd go to breakfast and then make a mysterious trip to the house. Liz hadn't been there since last Thursday, but she couldn't imagine what could have happened over the weekend that would put that silly smirk on Ethan's face. She loved her husband's "silly smirk," and he loved her sweet talk when she was trying to pry a secret out of him, so sweet-talk she would. She was feeling better this morning than she had in months. She wasn't sure what had lightened her spirit, but whatever it was; Ethan seemed to be on the same frequency. She was grateful. And right now, she was hungry…

He was deliberately taking the long way around, but she really didn't mind. It was encouraging to see buildings going up and trees being planted around their neighborhood; and besides, the weather this morning was absolutely amazing. In fact, the whole winter had been amazing. Almost as if that colossal storm had used up the year's full quota of bad weather, the climate had been remarkably mild, hardly calling for more than a sweater most of the time. Plants that normally didn't come alive for another month or so were already lush and blooming. Garden centers were beginning to stock early plants. Of course, there was no way she'd be able to plant anything this spring, but she could hardly wait to start getting her hands dirty in the fall. She already knew exactly what she wanted to do with the yard and what trees she wanted to plant around their new circle drive. By next spring, she fully intended that their yard would be full of butterflies again... the little, unintimidating ones, of course... the kind that hardly ever landed on a window.

At last they were here. Most of the outside work was done and she loved the way their house was coming together. It looked like they'd gotten the stone all finished on the porch. Finally! She was anxious to see it, but she'd been expecting that for weeks; so whatever the surprise was, it must be inside.

"Close your eyes and don't look until I say you can."

"What? What in the world are you..."

"Just close your eyes and give me your hand. Don't worry—I won't let you fall."

They walked slowly up the newly imprinted drive and across the stone porch, Liz obediently keeping her eyes closed, carefully feeling her way. They should be at the front door, she thought, but for some reason Ethan had stopped on the porch...

"Now! You can open your eyes."

Slowly she opened her eyes and looked around, then looked at Ethan, perplexed. The porch looked exactly as she'd hoped, so what...

"Down," he commanded. "Look down."

She complied and stood frozen, staring at the stone beneath her feet. It was her stone, retrieved from the neighbor's yard, shaped and cleaned and re-installed at their front door once again!

Out of the corner of her eye, Liz could see her husband watching her anxiously. She wanted to throw her arms around him and tell him how much this meant to her! That she'd never had a more precious gift! Her heart felt like it would explode with wonder at this man who still managed to amaze her after all these years, but if she dared to look at him she'd end up a hopeless puddle on that beautiful stone of remembrance. Then she saw the engraving at the top corner, three elegant butterflies soaring gracefully above the promise she still clung to, and she was overcome.

She fell to her knees, tears falling unrestrained, reverently tracing the words, *"I know the plans I have for you, says the LORD."*

Instantly he was beside her on the stone floor. "I'm so sorry I was such a jerk about this, Honey. I'm hoping this makes up for it a little."

Poor Ethan. She knew at times he just didn't know what to do with her. They'd always laughed that if one of them was going to cry at a sad movie it was probably going to be Ethan, but since the tornado it seemed that her first response to almost everything was tears. That evil wind that had blown away everything they owned seemed to have blown away everything Liz thought she was. Shakespeare's "ill wind" principle was certainly a reality in their lives.

Construction workers arrived that morning to find the owners of the house sitting on their new porch floor, leaning against their new front door, holding hands and chatting. Certainly that ill wind had blown away so much they cared about, but day by day they were beginning to see the good it was bringing. *"I know the plans I have for you, says the LORD"* would welcome them home as long as they lived in this house, and they knew the rest of the promise could be trusted. God's plans for their family were "good, and not for evil... to give [them] hope and a future."

22

The FIRST GLEAM of DAWN
TUESDAY, MAY 22, 2012

7:00 a.m.
Southwest Joplin, MO
McConnell Home

It was going to be a good day.

Elly stretched luxuriously and lay with her eyes closed, anticipating the day to come. She pulled her soft comforter over her shoulders and thought about everything that had happened since this moment exactly one year ago when she'd lingered in almost this same spot, listening to the same leaves rustling outside her window, looking forward to a very good day. She took a deep breath and slowly opened her eyes. It was almost scary. Same perfect sky—fresh and bright and blue with just a few fluffy white clouds. Same perfect sun, warm and soft across her bed. Same perfect leaves on the tree just outside her window, swaying in the morning breeze. *Her* tree... planted by her parents the day she was born, adorned by the prayers they etched there each year on her birthday, protected by the hand of God the day their world came apart.

She was glad her parents had decided to rebuild here, grateful they'd kept her room where it overlooked their "miracle trees," even though she would only be home a few weeks in the summers. Maybe "you can't go home again," she thought, but this sure felt like home. Mom and Dad had done such a good job of bringing the old and comfortable into their new, state-of-the-art home. Home! Incredible how good one word could sound. Amazing how important it was to know home was here for her as she worked at building her future.

Her mind drifted to the lovely basement patio in Carthage that had been her family's refuge in the worst storms of their lives. She'd been disappointed that she couldn't be there for the last dinner they'd shared with the Zimmerman's before they moved, but she was grateful that the comforter Ginny had bought her now graced her bed in her new room. It was a sweet connection to the inviting apartment that had been their home for nearly a year. She knew her family would not trade one moment there, as hard as some of it had been. They would especially miss the patio—it had been such a gift—but the fact was, it was still someone else's apartment in someone else's home.

Frank and Ginny had become so much a part of their family. It would be good to see them again today. As long as she could remember, Frank had been frail and sickly. Now it would be wonderful to see him healthy and energetic. Everyone said he hardly looked like the same man, but she knew that booming laugh and those twinkling eyes would never change. They all loved him so much, especially her little sister, and it was looking like there was every possibility his dream might become reality; that a grownup red-haired princess would someday kiss him "right there" for luck before she took her father's arm for that walk down the aisle.

It would be even better to see Big Pops and Gran. Gran had declared more than once that the freedom to spend more time with their grandchildren was just one step away from heaven, but they'd all been a little concerned that this big man who'd worked at ranching since he was a little boy would have a hard time adjusting to life without it. They needn't have worried. Sometime around Easter, Big Mike had challenged the depression that had haunted him after his heart attack in the same way he'd challenged unruly cattle for years—"head on." Since then, his flagging energy had returned and he was again his old dynamic self, dominating every room with his smile and joy for life.

Even in the busiest and hardest of times Pops had never lost sight of his commitment to disadvantaged children, and this summer Elly would be working with them to bring several "tornado kids" to northern Missouri for a week in the country. He and Beth were both having a ball with the gardens they'd created on the few acres they'd kept, Big Mike asserted. They'd never had time before to garden just for fun. He was so proud of his wife's creativity with her flower gardens—

it was already becoming legend among area gardeners—and he couldn't wait for the farmers' markets around the region to open. He was already signed up to sell produce from their truck gardens, and, ever the teacher, in his spare time he was working with farm co-ops to share with young ranchers and farmers what he'd learned over the years.

Elly stretched again, relishing the quiet. Better enjoy it now, she smiled to herself. The Little's would be storming up that new stairway any minute now. She thought about the pivotal moment last year when they'd snuggled in her bed and watched those amazing butterflies at her window. She couldn't help but feel a little nostalgic. They'd grown 'way too fast while she was gone, but she was so proud of them.

It was hard to believe Emma was four already, out-growing most of the baby talk they'd all thought was so cute. She smiled again as she thought of her little sister and her ever-present, much-loved Mary-Ann Maria Emmaleah, a bit bedraggled now from myriad tea parties and big wheel rides and naps and hugs and kisses.

And E.J.! Wise beyond his years, her little brother was seven-going-on-twenty-five, merry brown eyes now layered with the weight of all he'd seen and heard.

She loved them fiercely. How she wished she could build a wall that would protect them from it all. "OK, El, there you go again," she warned herself. "Must. Stop. Trying. To. Be. God!"

As they so often had since she'd moved into her new room, her eyes went again to the banner Mom had stenciled on the wall above her mirror: *"I know the plans I have for you, says the LORD. Plans for good and not for evil, to give you hope and a future." Jeremiah 29:11.* That scripture was such an awesome promise! It not only welcomed them through their front door every day, but she'd heard it quoted in more places than she could count this past year. She knew it had brought hope to so many in this disaster-haunted region, but it was still God's personal promise to her; to strengthen her in the hard times and remind her in the good that it is *His* plan He blesses the most.

"Thanks so much for being patient when I keep trying to be You, Lord," she whispered. "That's going to be our biggest struggle all my life, isn't it! I'm so glad You always win." It was just one more way she and her best friend were so different, Elly thought. She was certain Ali had gotten through one crisis after another since the storm with such strength and optimism because she was willing to trust God's plan instead of insisting on her own.

She would be here soon! They wanted—needed—to be part of events and memorials planned for this first-year anniversary of the day that changed their world forever. They talked and texted often, but they hadn't seen each other since Ali's surgery, and Elly could hardly wait. It had been good for them to spend their first year of college on their own. They'd grown in ways they probably wouldn't have if they'd had each other to lean on. But now Ali had decided she needed to move on from the painful memories that inhabited that year, and they were excited about attending the same university in August.

Though it had been troubling last February when they'd realized Alison would be facing more surgery, it had finally freed her from all the casts and braces and allowed her to start physical therapy. Typical of her ebullient friend, Ali was documenting every step of her recovery. It had taken all of Elly's willpower to look at the pictures she had emailed of her poor, shrunken arm, but at least it was straight now and the scars had actually gotten less noticeable as Ali worked at building up atrophied muscles. How lucky to have a friend like her, Elly thought, with such courage and spirit. How could she whine about anything when Ali had suffered so much and come out stronger and more hopeful than ever? She smiled. They'd been wiser than they'd known to make that pact about the nightmares. At first, those midnight calls had come several times a week. But, as Ali insisted Big Michael had promised, more and more their calls were in the light of day, to share some milestone, or celebrate some victory, or just to chat and giggle once again.

Her eyes fell on her chair, almost identical to the one she'd lost, picturing the leather folder that had rested there at this time a year ago. Now, the clothes she'd chosen to help face this day lay there instead. She wished she could have found that speech, but, oh well. Someone had posted they had a video of it. Maybe someday she'd track it down, but when so many of the really important things had been saved, how could she complain?

It was going to be a good day. But, she thought, very, very hard. Like many "tornado victors" with whom she'd talked, she anticipated the day with a mixture of excitement and anxiety. The media were back in force and as one heard in every venue; the eyes of the world were on their little Midwestern city again. In an age of "waiting for the helicopters to come," Joplin had endured the storm of the century with incredible faith and hope and gratitude and hard work and concern for each other. She was so proud of her town—so grateful their beautiful, historic downtown had been spared from the raging monster that had devastated much of their community. The city's leaders had spent the past ten years working hard to restore it to its earlier grace, and now it was a true metaphor for all that was right about this area. She loved being part of a culture that wasn't afraid to celebrate its heritage and publicly honor God.

The Governor couldn't have said it better a few minutes ago at the sunrise service: It *was* "...fitting to begin...by reflecting on our faith as dawn breaks over a renewed Joplin." It was true, Joplin *was* being renewed. Businesses and homes had already taken shape and many more were planned. Life and vitality were beginning to appear in the South Main Street region that had seemed so forsaken last year. Parks were still works in progress, but they would eventually be better than ever before; many with new, state-of-the-art playgrounds and aquatic areas. When she and Dad had taken that once-routine drive down Range Line yesterday, she'd been relieved to see old familiar landmarks like Wal-Mart and Home Depot, not so long ago the scene of appalling devastation and death, resplendent in their latest incarnations. Academy Sports would open again soon on the site where that ragged flag so bravely flew a year ago, and most of the businesses along the east side of Joplin's busiest thoroughfare were once again thriving.

The west side, however, was another matter. The site of the strip mall at 20th Street and other wrecked businesses along the next few blocks had been cleared; but sadly, very little re-building had begun. It was the same along 20th Street. A few new structures could be seen here and there, but mostly one saw only barren lots or stripped pads of concrete. She'd been surprised at the intensity of the disappointment she felt. Somehow, it seemed that only when the area was restored would she find the final healing of memories that still lived in the barrenness of that route.

She hadn't been able to face the Joplin High School graduation. Memories of last year and classmates who would not be there this year to celebrate were just too tender. Commendably, the Class of 2012 had made it through a senior year like no other in their unconventional school at the mall. Though the glare of national attention had brought accolades for their courage and resiliency, along with blessings like needed equipment and even prom dresses for all the girls, by the end of the year they mostly just longed for normalcy again.

She'd wanted to shout "yes!" this morning when the Governor had gone on to declare, "Scripture tells us that the path of the righteous is like the first gleam of dawn, shining ever brighter till the full light of day." It was true Joplin was being renewed, but today was, in fact, just "the first gleam of dawn." Even as her people longed to move on to a "new normal," they still struggled with the old. Some still faced years of grieving their losses before they would finally find peace in that new normal. Many still felt the unease of wishing they could do more, better, feeling it could never be enough. And she knew from her own experiences, very few would not struggle at one time or another with questions for which there were no answers.

Slight movement at the window caught her eye. A chill touched her spine. She and Mom had just joked yesterday that they'd finally conquered their "butterfly phobia," but this was much too déjà vu! Her mind's eye saw three enormous butterflies at her window once again, harbingers of disaster on "a very good day." She took a deep breath and forced herself to look. Then she laughed out loud. A hummingbird! No, three hummingbirds, delicate wings a blur as they hovered at the flower-shaped feeder someone had hung at her window! Their fragile beauty glistened in the sunlight. Like butterflies at her window, they seemed a living promise that whatever might come, this was going to be a very good day indeed. Then, almost like an asterisk accenting the promise, one small, bright butterfly settled on the bird feeder and sat, wings outspread as if in benediction.

A thousand emotions and memories swirled through her. She slowly rose from bed and crept to the window. She needn't have been so cautious. The birds were much too focused on the nectar they'd discovered in that convenient flower, and the butterfly remained so still it could have been a part of the feeder itself. She sat at the window, studying it. So much had happened since that butterfly moment a year ago, but the image of those three incredible creatures was engraved in her mind forever. This one was a small but exact replica of the one she thought of as "Big Michael's" alter ego. Was it just a coincidence? Or could it be her loving Father's little reminder that His plan for her truly was "hope and a future?"

She decided yes, her God was big enough to use the smallest tools for His purpose. She loved the idea that one small butterfly could be His messenger of hope to a worn and weary family.

Well, she'd better stop daydreaming and get ready. Ali would be breezing through her door any minute and she'd be merciless if Elly wasn't ready to go. She thought her friend must keep a running tally of who was late last. She had to admit, it was one of the qualities they definitely did not share. Ali was almost always early, while Elly… well…

Reluctantly, she resisted burrowing back under the covers, disappointed her little brother and sister hadn't joined her there. She loved those special mornings when they snuggled together, sharing their questions and dreams and hopes for the day. She wondered what they were feeling about this day. She knew their counselor had decided they were healthy enough now to release them, and she agreed. She could see it in their eyes. But as necessary and exciting as this day of remembrance and celebration was to everyone in the area, it was going to be hard for all of them. She faced the day with a mixture of longing for it to go on and on, and a desire to see it become tomorrow.

Tomorrow all the front-page stories would be written and the media would be off to the next big disaster; and her people would go back to replanting and rebuilding and restoring fragmented lives. She knew her friends and neighbors were more than ready for a better tomorrow... a new normal. Soon they would be having conversations that didn't include storm stories. One day they would no longer panic at dark clouds they used to relish. But when the eyes of the world were no longer on Joplin, MO, would their new normal still be a more caring, compassionate community than ever before? When it was no longer "life-or-death-on-the-evening-news," would they still choose their neighbor's good over their own? Would they, like Tuscaloosa, put aside their own struggles to go and serve where they were needed? A year from now, behind the undaunted crosses and flying flags and smiley faces, would they still show the world a mid-western spirit that could not be broken? Would the world still look at her community and say, "There's something different about Joplin?" And when they did, would Joplin still give honor and praise to the One who made all the difference?

"Yes," she thought, "there really was something different about Joplin, and with God's help, yes, they would!"

EPILOGUE

While characters in this book are strictly fictional except for quotes from Missouri's governor, landmarks are real and stories are rooted in actual experiences of Joplin tornado survivors and volunteers.

College Heights Christian Church immediately appointed leadership and developed programs, closed its school for the year and made all its resources available for tornado relief. The church has continued to play a pivotal role in helping the community heal.

"Amanda" was inspired by a courageous young single mom named Andrea who drove the one hundred fifty miles from Kansas City with only her little girl's pup tent and limited resources because "God told her to do something." I met her as we were evacuating the church on that frightening Tuesday after the storm and brought her home to stay with us the next few nights. We still stay in touch...

"Outreach House" is loosely modeled on Watered Gardens, a ministry to the homeless in downtown Joplin.

Uncounted families in this area who made their homes and belongings available to tornado survivors and volunteers are epitomized by "the Zimmerman's."

Some stories are very personal. Our family was one of many that celebrated a graduate's success in a South Range Line restaurant right before that monstrous EF5 tornado hit. Our just-graduated Marine-recruit grandson Eli, his older brother Seth, and their buddies were among those who walked back into "the belly of the beast" to search and rescue and see things that still haunt their thoughts.

My husband and I are just one of myriad "what if" stories: What if we had not decided to drop by our daughter's home just south of the tornado's path before we started toward our home northwest of Joplin? We would have driven straight into the teeth of the storm!

It was our son-in-law Jim who miraculously rode out the tornado in a Duquesne Village alley. He had gone to try to check on our granddaughter Carissa as the storm moved in.

My husband and our daughter Kim maneuvered our SUV through streets littered with rubble and fallen electric lines, to try to find Jim and reach Carissa, as Ethan did hunting Elly, and hers is one of those miracle stories of choosing to move her children at the last moment to the only place in her house where they could have survived. It was her nine-year-old son Gabriel who warned his mother about a broken gas line and later explained matter-of-factly that they'd prayed REALLY LOUD and God told him to warn her, of course. His eleven-year-old sister Lillian really did find her bunny hopping through the ruins of their house unharmed, its smashed cage high on a shelf. All fifteen of her baby chicks actually were found alive under their wrecked house, still in their cage. And their three-year-old sister Kayleah, even though she was traumatized, understood right away that God had saved them and told everyone who would listen.

They know first-hand the struggle to overcome nightmares and heal memories and reclaim a sense of security and normalcy, but Carissa writes, "… this was like a horrible forest fire that devastates everything, but out of it comes new growth, that flourishes, and a newness of life. People have come from all over to help and it has been life changing and restores my faith in humanity and compassion and love for others, it is amazing."

Chronicles of "butterfly people" abound. Whether you believe they could be guardian angels sent by God; some supernatural manifestation; or simply figments of fear and trauma and wishful thinking will depend on how, and if, you believe "God governs in the affairs of men." Unquestionably amazing things occurred on May 22, 2011, that cannot be explained by human reasoning.

Joplin is still being rebuilt and renewed. Volunteers are still returning to help. Units in the "FEMA villages" are being moved out as people find new homes. "Extreme Home Makeover" celebrated their closing shows with seven new homes for tornado families, and Habitat for Humanity and other charities continue to build several houses at a time. St. John's Hospital is now Mercy Hospital Joplin with completion of their new, state-of-the-art campus on the southeast outskirts of Joplin projected for 2015. New schools are under construction. Trees have been planted and devastated parks rebuilt; and thousands came together on May 22, 2012, to join the Unity Walk and celebrate the hope and future they've been given.

Now, the hardest work has begun—that long, slow, not-so-glamorous slog toward a new, improved normal that will take years to achieve. Statistics show the next few years will be dangerous. When celebrity is gone and life becomes daily again, then marital abuse rises and children become angry and families fall apart and post-traumatic shock takes its toll. Will Joplin still be different then? Still continue to defy the odds? I think, as Elly says, with God's help, yes! You see, that's what is different about Joplin. God is here.

END of BOOK 1

THE STORY CONTINUES in BOOK 2
of MIRACLES in the STORM

Standpipes & Storm Shelters is "the rest of the story" of *Butterflies at the Window*. It is the account of the Morris family, still struggling to find hope after most victims of the Joplin Tornado have found homes and jobs and healing. It is the on-going saga of the McConnell's commitment to use all that happened to them to bless others. But most of all, it is the testimony of God's faithful pursuit of those He loves, even when they don't want to know Who He is.

A SNEAK PEAK at

STANDPIPES and STORM SHELTERS

BOOK 2 of MIRACLES In The STORM
Excerpt Copyright © 2016 by Sandi McReynolds
Published by VineTree Press

STANDPIPES and STORM SHELTERS

(From Chapter 1 of *Standpipes and Storm Shelters*)

Jax stood in the open door, leaning on the cane he despised, grimly surveying his surroundings. Nothing left as far as he could see, he thought bitterly, except those blasted abandoned standpipes and ugly useless storm shelters.

He'd hated those unsightly concrete boxes since he'd first seen them two years ago. They were a painful, in-your-face reminder that Jax Morris was as vulnerable as any man. He still shuddered to think of the terrifying night that had taught him that lesson. In less than a heartbeat a monstrous storm had turned their pleasant, ordered world into chaos and he hadn't even been able to protect himself, let alone the people he loved most. For the first time in his life, he'd been helpless and afraid.

Jaxon James Morris II was a man's man, even more rugged and burly than the father he'd idolized. Like his father, he was proud of his blue-collar heritage. The skills J. J. Morris had taught him as a teen-ager in Michigan had always been his strength and identity and he'd loved to boast that he was just like his father. They both could work and fight and drink any man under the table, he often declared to any who would listen. Unlike his father, however, he'd found his greatest meaning in his family. He loved them fiercely.

He'd adored beautiful, dark-haired Marianna Guarino since grade school. As a young bride, she'd been patient with his need to unwind with the guys after work, but when Jaxon James III was born, followed by Edward Roy two years later, evenings at the bar with the guys had eagerly become evenings at home with his guys.

Shortly after the sudden death of his father he'd moved his young family to Southwest Missouri where he hoped he'd find relief from the lingering ache in his heart. It had been a good move. There, his plumbing business had flourished. There, Marianna had cheerfully set about making their new house a home and the boys had found new friends. And there, Angelina Marianna had graced their lives. His little Angel was a blue-eyed, blond-haired throwback to the Morris clan's Scots heritage and Jax had found himself more madly in love than he'd ever thought possible. Surely no man had ever been so favored by whatever gods decided such things.

All that had changed on May 22, 2011. The EF5 tornado that struck their adopted town would quickly be labeled "the storm of the century." It had taken only twenty minutes for the mile-wide monster to roar through the city, but it had left the Morris's and thousands of other families devastated and homeless. Now his children struggled with the night, still haunted by the terror of that dark time. Now their father struggled with the day, still facing months of therapy on his shattered leg, still hoping it would eventually support him without this blasted cane, still fearful he might never work again. Now, they no longer enjoyed the friendly, middle-class neighborhood where their newly-remodeled home had anchored their lives. Since that fateful night, they'd simply survived in the sweeping "FEMA Village" that had sprung up northwest of the city.

As soon as FEMA had secured the site across from the old municipal airport, the agency had built those huge, unappealing concrete shelters; positioning them strategically throughout the project and around the outer perimeter; adding temporary housing units as tornado survivors were approved for them. Most of the displaced families living there were truly grateful. Having a home—even a featureless, temporary one—made rebuilding shattered lives seem somehow possible and the storm shelters helped restore a sense of security that had been cruelly blown away. Even so, one could hardly help but be depressed by such dreary surroundings. Not a tree or blade of grass remained in what had once been flourishing hay fields. Now those cheerless acres were crisscrossed by narrow streets lined by row after mind-numbing row of identical rectangles looking for all the world like drab little white mobile homes without wheels.

At least their unit was at the very back of the project, Jax had consoled himself. He'd rather look at trailers than those awful storm shelters. One by one, though, as families relocated to the homes and apartments that were being rebuilt, the uninviting rectangles had begun disappearing. Now, only a few scattered modules remained. This morning the trailer across the street had been moved out, leaving the Morris's isolated in a network of empty drives and deserted electrical standpipes. Word was that the storm shelters would eventually be sold to local organizations, but for now they dominated barren fields that had once been teeming with the wounded community in which they'd become unwilling participants.

He should call Marianna. He knew she was hurting as much as he was, though she seemed to have found some comfort in her new friends. He was not at all happy with the idea that his wife had become a church goer, but he had to admit he was a little surprised—even disappointed maybe?—that she'd never asked him to go with her.

He couldn't blame her for leaving, though. In fact, he'd been relieved when she'd taken the kids and moved to that Zimmerman place in Carthage. This rage that consumed him now terrified him even more than it had her, and at least there they had the peace and security he could no longer give them. What probably scared him even more, though, was that he seldom even missed them. If he dared allow any emotion at all into his big frame, he could risk only the anger that drove him.

His hand tightened on the head of his cane as a big white SUV turned off Highway 171 and headed his way. Ethan! His first impulse was to close the door and pretend he wasn't here. He had to admit at times it helped to feel like at least one person in this miserable world remembered he existed; but he still couldn't figure out why this man who seemed to have everything going for him was so determined to connect with him.

At first he'd thought it was some sort of "survivor guilt," like they'd talked about in those first sessions of disaster relief counseling. (He probably should have made sure his family stayed in that program longer, but it seemed like he'd come home from every session angrier than before they'd gone and Marianna had refused to go without him.)

Then he'd found out Ethan's family had been through even more than his, so he'd decided maybe the guy was one of those do-gooders who insisted on sticking their noses in other people's business. But if that was all it was, why would he keep coming back; even when Jax was downright rude at times? It seemed like no matter what he did, Ethan just wouldn't give up. Finally he'd had to admit he wanted that friendship. Whether he liked it or not, this man he couldn't begin to understand had become his only real ally in this strange new world.

His ruddy face colored a deep red as he remembered the first time he'd met the McConnell family. Those poor kids were so excited about bringing Thanksgiving baskets to people in the Village, but he'd been outright nasty and slammed the door in their faces. The idea of someone offering his family a handout had felt like the final blow to his manhood. He knew that didn't excuse bad manners, though. Ethan insisted he understood, but Jax still felt embarrassed about it. He'd have been furious if someone had treated his kids that way. But they'd just left the box at the door and quietly disappeared. Marianna had found a note Ethan had scribbled to him in the bottom of the box: "We'll be praying for your family this holiday season. Believe it or not, I really do understand what you're going through, and I know God has a plan in all this heartache. I'll try to catch you in a week or so. I think we have a lot to talk about."

"Yeah, right," he'd thought bitterly. "I can already see we have so much in common."

Actually, he'd been shocked that they did have a lot in common. Ethan's wife and kids had been trapped in the tornado, too, and he'd struggled with the same helpless panic that haunted Jax. According to Ethan, they'd worked through his dad's heart attack and his wife's paralysis; then the little ones' nightmares and his older daughter's guilt and grief before he'd realized the toll it was taking. He'd eventually broken, and their marriage had been falling apart when they'd finally gotten help from some trusted friends.

Why would a man like Ethan share all that with anyone? It did sound a lot like his story, but he still couldn't bring himself to risk trusting anyone, even Ethan McConnell. He was glad Marianna had been able to, though—glad she'd found something good in her life—but their so-called God would sure never bother with a guy like him. Especially when he'd spent his whole life denying he even existed.

ABOUT THE AUTHOR

Sandi McReynolds is a life-long resident of Southwest Missouri. As the monstrous Joplin tornado carved its way across the region, her family and friends found themselves in its grip. "Butterflies at the Window" is based on their true experiences and the mysterious butterfly people stories that followed.

www.ingramcontent.com/pod-product-compliance
Lightning Source LLC
Chambersburg PA
CBHW060043150626
46556CB00018BA/2677